GW00381468

MADE IN
BRITAIN

MADE IN BRITAIN

Gavin James Bower

QUARTET

First published in 2011 by
Quartet Books Limited
A member of the Namara Group
27 Goodge Street, London W1T 2LD

A catalogue record for this book
is available from the British Library

ISBN   978 0 7043 7229 0

Typeset by Antony Gray
Printed and bound in Great Britain by
T J International Ltd, Padstow, Cornwall

PART ONE

CHAPTER ONE

Russell

I could love you.

I pass a girl crossing the canal on my way home. It's dark but our eyes meet, and there's a connection.

We could talk, I think. We could laugh.

We could spit on the heads of imaginary tourists taking boat trips along the water below us. They'd have to be imaginary, of course, because nobody ever visits here.

I live on Every Street, in a town that's so common it might as well be called Every Town. Half of the houses on our road are boarded up, the Asians are taking over and the only shop isn't even a shop; it's a Co-op Funeral Care. It used to be a pub before the landlord, a man called Dorian who liked dressing up as a cowboy, got arrested for masturbating over a guest's face while he was asleep.

I want you, I think as the girl walks away from me. I want you to want me.

I want you to creep up behind me while I'm sitting at my desk, doing homework, and wrap your arms around my neck.

I want you to whisper my name.

'*Russell . . .* '

My granddad always used to tell me that I should be an artist, because of my name. It's Russell Crackle. Apparently Dad was a bit of an eccentric when he was younger, spending all his time reading books and listening to music in his room. He had his name changed by Deed Poll when he was 21. Mum never bothered to change it when he left us, because you have to pay.

I walk down the grassy embankment and up the main road that leads to my house, passing what used to be Lambert Howarth. By the time she was my age Mum had left school and got her first job there, but it's closed now.

Life is transient, I think as I walk through my front door. But love, well, love is different.

Love is forever.

Charlie

Jenny's passed out on my lap, a bottle of White Lightning in her cold, pale hand.

I'm up the canal, and can see the whole town from where I'm sitting. The old mills to my left, the rows of terraced houses boarded up now on that side of town, and the council blocks where Trafalgar Flats used to be, before they knocked them down. Straight ahead's the new bus station, lit up in purple. To my right's the new sports centre, which used to be the multi-storey, and next to that's the new multi-storey, which used to be the sports centre.

I take the bottle from Jenny, chuck it under the bench, and pull her close to keep her warm. I stroke her hair and she smiles, half asleep.

'Am I drunk?' she asks, her eyes closed.

'Back in a sec,' I say, after she doesn't say owt else, then, smiling to myself, 'don't go anywhere, love . . . '

I climb over the wall behind us and piss in the canal, my

back to town, the abandoned train track in front of me. Brooker and Digger are slumped against the wall. Nicola's with them, fumbling with a baggie. She looks fucked.

'Lend us a fag,' I say, coming up behind them.

'Fuck *me*!" Brooker shouts. 'Yer scared shit outta me!'

Brooker likes snorting speed and getting into scraps. He goes to my school and we've knocked about since day one. I met him when he was going round cuffing everyone with a fifty pence piece. I thought it was funny, at the time. He's only small, Brooker, but he's from Stoops Estate so knows a thing or two about fighting. He plays football for school and Centre of Excellence, like me. He was top scorer this season, but he's best known for kicking the shit out of people on the pitch. In our last game, against St Ted's, he tackled this lad so hard he ended up being carried off and needing bolts and pins and that in his leg. He might be a scrawny fucker but he's scared of no one, the little knob.

He stands up, hands me one.

'Got a light?' I ask, looking at Nicola. She tries to line up some ket on a pocket mirror, but spills it. I look back at Brooker as he rummages in his pockets then lights my fag for me. 'You should take her home, you tight cunt.' I stare at him, so he knows I mean it. 'She's spinnin' out.'

'OK OK,' he says. 'We were only 'avin' a bit o' fun – '

'I'm fuckin' off anyway,' I interrupt. I'm tired and not in the mood to get into an argument with him. 'I'm gonna take Jenny home . . . '

'Yer comin' out tomorro'?' Digger asks, chopping up what's left of the K.

Digger likes Brooker and getting into scraps. He goes to my school and all and I don't remember when I met him but, for as long as I can remember, wherever Brooker was he was too. He's stocky and tough, the kind of lad you'd describe as being carved out of wood.

'Prolly,' I say, even though I know full well I will be.

I walk Jenny home. She lives just up from the canal, about fifteen minutes, but it takes twice that 'cause she's falling all over the shop, deadweight. It's only when she hugs me on her front step I realise she could've walked quicker, and without my help.

'In a bit,' I say, not wanting to linger.

'Why d'yer waste yer time wi' us lot?' she says, holding my hand and hugging me.

'What d'you mean?' I say as she pulls me in, tight. Her hair smells like strawberries and cider.

'Those two . . . *knobs*,' she says, slurring her words a bit. 'Why d'yer hang round wi' 'em? Why d'yer waste yer time . . . wi' us . . . wi' *me*?'

'I dunno,' I say, trying to get away again. 'It's a laugh . . . '

'Yer think yer too good for me, don't yer?' she says, a bit OTT, pulling me back towards her again then kissing me hard on the mouth.

I step back and look at her. It's sloppy but she tastes nice, of vanilla chapstick, so I pull her back into me and shag her right there, against her front door, just to shut her up.

Hayley
Dad knocks on the door to tell me I've got a brew waiting

on the landing. I live with him 'cause my mum died of lung cancer when I was thirteen. He does his best, but I miss her loads.

Every night before bed I lock the bathroom door and sneak a ciggy on the loo, freezing my tits off with the window open so Dad doesn't catch me. I'll be dead if he does. Then I take a long shower to warm up again. Sometimes, I sit down in the bath and let the water hit me in the chest until it turns so red I look like a lobster when I get out. But tonight I just let the spray hit me in the face.

I've been for a walk up the canal with Gemma, my best friend, and all this eyeliner what she gave me is running down my face and drip-dripping at my feet. I stare down at my piggy toes – I hate my feet 'cause they're so massive, well, size six, which I reckon is massive for my age – and watch the black swirling its way down the plughole.

I usually have a good cry in the shower, 'specially when I'm missing Mum. Now's no different, but I soon start singing to cheer myself up again. She always used to say life's more fun with a song, and I should belt one out every chance I get. Tonight it's 'Daydream Believer'. Mum's favourite.

I only get through one verse, though, before Dad taps on the door again, telling me my brew's going cold. I can't sing when I know people are listening.

'OK Dad,' I say, stepping out then grabbing my hairbrush. 'Cheer up, sleepy Jean . . . ' I mime into it. 'Oh, what can it mean, to a . . . daydream believer, and a . . . homecoming queeeeeeeeeeeeeeeeeen?'

CHAPTER TWO

Russell

It's been just the two of us for a while now, Mum and me, but I've been arguing with her a lot lately and we had another falling out this morning.

I needed a clean shirt for school and there wasn't one. When I went into her bedroom to tell her, she got really mad, shouting at me because I'd disturbed her and she was having her lie-in. She always has a lie-in. She stays in all day and can't even be bothered to wash me a shirt every once in a while. I just said that I was sorry, though – I don't know what for – and left the house with a dirty shirt on.

On my way to the station, I see two rough lads hugging aggressively at a vandalised bus stop. They catch me looking and start shouting, but I quicken my stride and, luckily, they don't end up chasing me.

I seem to spend half the time daydreaming, and the other half being scared to death. The fact that I live next to a funeral parlour doesn't help. It's a reminder of my own mortality, you know, the need to leave something behind – but I can't seem to decide what that something will be.

It used to be all so different. Lying on the school fields at lunchtime. The smell of freshly cut grass. Pervasive. Verdant. Words I didn't know existed. But I didn't care.

You, me, carefree.

The boys would pick up piles of cut grass left by the mower and throw them at the girls. When they weren't looking up their skirts. Between their legs. Smooth thighs. Pale and soft.

I noticed legs before breasts. Hoisted skirts, rolled up three times to show off these newly discovered assets, with white socks on supple and shapely calves.

Bulge. If glimpsed, bulge was the Holy Grail. You can look but you can't touch. I didn't have a clue what to do even if I *was* allowed to touch – I still don't – but that wasn't the point. That was scary. To look, to glimpse a girl's knickers between toned thighs, was enough.

When did enough stop being enough.

Charlie

It's just gone eight and two girls are staggering up Manny Road, taking turns to swig from a bottle of vodka. One of them throws the empty bottle against a boarded up doss house.

I'm on my way to the station to catch the school bus. Walking down the hill towards town, tired from the late one last night, I pass that pinhead who works at Sainsbury's collecting trolleys. He stares at me in a weird way, so I stare back until he looks away.

I meet Brooker and Digger in the station but they're acting like dicks, trying to pick a fight with some Ivy Bank lads – Ivy Wankers, they call them. I see the bus pull in so leave them to it.

The seating plan on the school bus is all about knowing your place. It's fairly straight-forward, and understood by school kids everywhere. The hardest and most popular go to the back, the quiet, brooding types by the window and the gobbiest and probably softest in the middle, maybe with their feet on the seats in front. Then there are those seats that make you face someone. These are for less popular lads or sometimes the fittest girls, 'cause they're still close to the back and the top of the tree. Then there's everywhere else, which is divided up first-come, first-served. But remember, the closer the front you get the lower you are in the food chain, so choose wisely or you might get battered.

I sit down at the back in my usual seat, by the window. There are three girls from my year and two Third Year lads sitting in front of me.

'You got Fifa yet?' one of the lads asks the other.

'No but I've ordered it. My mum said I could get it yesterday, but Asda were sold out . . . '

'Even on PS2?'

'No, on PS3, X-Box and DS. Have you got it?'

'Yeah I started a career yesterday. I made myself for Accrington Stanley.'

'How much?'

'I traded in all my other games. That came to thirty-two quid, so it only cost me eight.'

'That's alreet. I've heard the shots are realistic now . . . '

'Yeah I like it when you tackle. They don't just fall over no more. And they proper slide for ages!'

I stop listening as this bloke gets on. His name's Seth, a supply teacher at school, but he looks proper young, about eighteen. He's wearing a shirt and tie, filthy jeans, a black leather trench coat and sunglasses. He shouldn't be allowed on, but he seems to know the driver.

'Reet,' he says, nodding his head and pointing at me, like his hand's a gun.

He sits down next to me at the back, in the middle, and puts his feet on the seats in front. His teeth are all chipped and stained, his hair's greasy, and his skin's grey with a bit of yellow in it.

'I'm DJin' at Xstasy t'neet,' he carries on, after I turn away to look out the window. 'Hoping this Sixth Former comes and all. She gave me her number after class . . . '

He gets off at the stop before school. As the bus drives away he points at me again, this time pulling the trigger.

Hayley

'What job does your dad do?' Laura asks. Laura's well annoying but Gemma likes her, so I put up with her on the way to school every day.

'He's an upholsterer,' I say, looking out the window.

Really Dad does two jobs. He's an upholsterer at the local firm, but his hours keep getting cut back so he's taken a part-time job mending cars. He's always saying, 'Hayley my lass, business has gone for a shite round 'ere' – but I don't really know what that means. All I know is, he works non-stop and I hardly ever see him.

I get why, course. Dad's always been the one out working, and he told me I'm not allowed to get a part-time job or owt, even though I turned sixteen this year. He wants it to stay the same as it was, before Mum died, but I just wish we spent more time together.

I'm going Drama school next year, though, so maybe one day I'll be famous and able to look after him. I just want to make him proud.

'What does he upholster?' she carries on, for some reason giggling – silly cow.

'Dunno,' I say. We're sitting on those seats what make you face someone and I'm looking straight at Laura, so I'm finding it hard to ignore her. 'Owt really . . . '

'Like cats?'

'And postmen?' Gemma pipes up. I give her evils but she just winks at me.

'And, like, Ford Escorts?'

We pull into the bus station and there's a change of driver, which takes ages 'cause the big butch one, who's getting on, chats away like it's going out of fashion to the Paki one who's getting off.

Then I see Charlie. I really fancy him, even though we've barely spoken in all five years of school. He's got nice skin and mean eyes, and looks proper hard. He's got big hands, too, which Gemma says is a sign he's got a big willy. Not that I'd know a big one if he lobbed it out right there at the front of the bus. I'm a virgin, and everybody knows it.

Charlie's not a virgin. Far from it. Rumour has it he lost it to a lady copper who'd caught him throwing stones at some gypo's caravan. He was thirteen.

Brooker and Digger get on next, and start pinging sweets at two Third Year boys sitting next to us. Then they sit down at the front. I lean to my right so I can see past Laura's fat head – she's proper skinny with a big head, so big she looks like a lollipop – and I notice they've surrounded that weird boy Russell.

'Hug a hoodie!' Brooker shouts from the seat behind him, putting his arm round Russell's neck and pulling his head back. Digger starts laughing. 'Don't worry,' Brooker carries on, 'we're not gonna hurt yer . . . '

'He's pissed himself!' a girl, who's just got on, shouts from the front. Brooker and Digger just laugh. 'No seriously,' she says, now standing next to them and laughing her head off too. 'He's actually pissed himself!'

CHAPTER THREE

Russell

I'm sitting on a bench in the park, trying to forget about this morning by watching a girl from school taking photos. I didn't realise, until now, but she's really quite pretty. Not in an obvious way. No, she's pretty because she's different.

She's pretty because she reminds me of you.

I did a project with her in Year Seven, for English. We'd been paired together and I got her mobile number, in case we had to work on it after school. I've never had the courage to text her and she's probably changed her number since then, but she actually smiled at me earlier today. I think she's a virgin too, so maybe I have a chance.

Well, probably not, but at least she noticed me.

Right now she's capturing a garden from every conceivable angle. I'm capturing her too, in my mind. She adjusts her camera. Click. She kneels in the middle of a path leading up to a fountain. Click. She wanders between some trees, carefully altering her stride to find the best possible point of view. Click.

These are the negatives in my mind, created by my photographic memory to be sifted through at a later date, in moments of recollection and reflection.

I have to get back to school soon but an older woman sits next to me on the bench. She opens a book and I decide to linger, to remain in the here and now.

'You look sad,' I say to her, after a while.

'Sorry?' she says, glancing at me, her sunglasses still on.

'You look sad,' I say again, this time louder. The sun has disappeared behind a cloud, the coward, and it's gone cold. The woman wraps herself in her cardigan. 'Are you OK?'

'Do I know you?' she says, turning to face me, her tone slightly menacing, if you can be a menace but only a bit of one.

'No, but we could change that,' I say, edging closer on the bench so there's nothing between us. 'What do you do?'

'I spend all my time in parks talking to strange men,' she answers, deadpan. 'And you?'

'I spend all my time in parks talking to strange women,' I say, smiling. 'And all just to go to bed with them. After all's said and done.'

'Would you like to go to bed with me?' she asks, the beginnings of a saucy grin visible in the corners of her mouth.

'Yes I would,' I answer. 'I would like that very much.'

Charlie

Brooker and Digger are waiting for me outside Maths, but they jog on when I bump into Ishtiaq. He puts his arm round me, says he wants a word.

We go outside to the car park and I see Asif waiting in front of a black X5. He dropped out last year, but I still see him knocking about round school. He's skinny with lines shaved in his eyebrows, gobby, and full of it. Over-compensating, I reckon.

'You alreet then Charlie lad?' Ish asks, shaking hands with Asif. He's got a broad accent, Ish, which always makes me laugh. He says summat to Asif, who then gets in this black X5. It's got tinted windows so I can't make out the driver. 'I need t' go t' shop,' he carries on. 'Walk wi' me.'

We walk in silence. I don't know him well so there's nowt much to say. I suppose I respect him, maybe only 'cause he's hard. He probably feels the same way about me, to be fair.

'Yer gettin' a job in t' summer then?' he asks as he comes out the chippy, holding just a can of Coke.

'I dunno really . . . '

I need to find summat, that's for sure. My dad's on at me to start contributing at home, so I'll have to work over summer. Fuck knows what I'll do after that.

'I haven't sorted owt out yet.'

'I'm not gonna mess yer 'bout Charlie lad,' he says, turning to face me. 'Yer know what goes down. I know yer not thick. Thing is, we're expandin' and, well . . . the boss wants t' meet yer . . . ' He stops and takes a swig from his Coke. I'm not sure where he's going with this, but keep it shut. 'If yer interested, like, come down Power-house Gym, any Sunday, and we'll talk.'

'I dunno Ish,' I say, after a bit. I do pills and that, but nowt else, and Ish is into much stronger stuff. 'It's not summat I've – '

'Just think about it,' he interrupts. 'If yer wanna know more, come down Sunday. If not, no 'ard feelings, alreet?' He holds out his hand.

'Alreet,' I say, shaking it.

Hayley

I'm taking photos in the park at dinner. Dad bought me a little digital camera for my birthday 'cause I'd told him I wanted to be a photographer, like Annie Liebovitz. That was before I watched summat on *GMTV* the other week and realised she's a shrivelled up lezzer. I promised him I'd get some use out of it, though, so am just pointing it at owt really. Once I fill up the memory card and get them developed – and he sees how rubbish I am – he'll get over it.

I must've taken a million pictures now, and am starving. I haven't eaten owt all day 'cause I've been feeling really fat lately. When I'm with Gemma, who's dead podgy, I always feel nice and thin. But now she only ever wants to hang round with that stick insect Laura. I feel a right fat cow next to her.

I walk to the shop and see Charlie talking to Ishtiaq. I wish he wouldn't hang round with that lot. Everyone knows all those Pakis in flash cars are dealing drugs. They'll just get him into trouble, but he's better than them. He's in the top set and did well good in his Mocks. I barely passed mine, *and* I revised loads.

Oh well. Perhaps I'll be a famous photographer after all, and get paid millions to snap gorgeous models. Or footballers. Yeah, I could take pictures of footballers when they pose for those sexy calendars. Snapping away at Cristiano Ronaldo with his shirt off would suit me down to the ground, I reckon.

I make my way back to school. Jenny Super Slag Catlow and that lot are sitting on the wall across the road. They all look the same, shirts un-tucked and half-open so their boobs are on show, skirts rolled up about five times and so much fake tan on their legs they end up orange.

That pramface Sally Lockyer's there, too. She had to drop out 'cause she got up the duff and she's got it with her now, poor little thing.

I look down at my feet as I pass, but it goes quiet and I know they'll all bitch about me when I'm out of earshot. Probably about me being a virgin. They call me frigid just 'cause I haven't opened my legs for some lad, but what do I care?

I walk through the car park and see Mr Mitchell, who teaches English Lit. He's struggling to carry his papers and lock his car door at the same time. He's young, for a teacher, and quite cute in a random way.

'D'you want a hand, sir?'

'Oh, erm, yes please . . . ' he says, pushing his glasses back off the end of his nose and turning to face me. 'Hayley, isn't it?'

'Yes, sir,' I say, taking the pile of papers off him. I don't have Mr Mitchell anymore 'cause I'm not in the top set, but I had him in first year. 'What are all these?'

'Old exam papers. Would you like to take one? They're for the Advanced examination, but it wouldn't hurt.' He pushes his glasses back off his nose again and smiles sheepishly.

'Thanks a lot, sir,' I say, helping myself to one.

I feel embarrassed walking side by side with him. Not 'cause he's a teacher – like I say, he's quite nice actually – but 'cause he probably thinks I'm a right dunce.

'I'll take them from here,' he says as we reach the main doors. 'Thank you again, Hayley.'

'No problem, sir,' I say, smiling then looking down. I know I'll have gone red. I always do.

'You know,' he says, turning back to face me in the doorway, 'you could come for a cramming session, after school . . . if you think you'd benefit from it. I know you're doing the Foundation examination, but there's always the chance for you to be promoted to Advanced, with a bit of extra effort on your part . . . as well as help on mine, of course – '

'Sir I'd love to!' I blurt out.

I need to do as well as I can in the exams or I'll never get into Drama school – and it'll be McDonald's for me. The only way I'd end up famous then would be as one of those real life stories in celeb mags, y'know, weighing forty stone and pregnant with triplets.

'I mean, that would be really helpful,' I carry on, trying to sound a bit less crazy. What a numpty.

'OK then,' he says, smiling. 'See you after school.'

I turn round, beaming. Until I see Jenny Catlow and that lot standing right in front of me. They're all smirking.

'I 'ope you told 'im yer under lock and key down there,' Jenny says, laughing and pointing between her legs. She brushes past in the doorway, bumping into me. 'Oops! Dint see yer there . . . '

CHAPTER FOUR

Russell

I'm sitting in a cubicle, my head in my hands. It's nearly five and I've been here since school finished, but I didn't want to catch the bus with everyone else.

I think there's someone in the cubicle next to me. It was locked when I came in and there's a lot of shuffling around going on but I daren't look over, or under, in case they catch me.

I look up at the back of the cubicle door, and consider the blank surface in front of me. Removing a red marker pen from my top pocket, I write *L'émancipation de l'homme sera totale ou ne sera pas* in large letters, slap bang in the middle of the door. It's a slogan from the 1968 protests in Paris, which I found on the internet and memorised. It means, 'The liberation of humanity will be total or it will not be.'

I think about this afternoon in the park, when I sat silently, no more than a metre away from that older woman on the bench. I was thinking of asking her, in a roundabout way, if she'd like to have sex. We exchanged glances when we were sure the other wasn't looking. But that was the extent of our connection. A connection conjured only in the mind of a virgin.

I'm usually so good with words. At least, when it comes to writing. My granddad, who's the only person I've ever shown my writing to, used to say that I must have

25

swallowed a dictionary. When it comes to actually talking to people, though, I'm useless. Words literally fail me.

Was she thinking what I was thinking, though, and just too scared to say it out loud? Was she pretending to read her book while actually picturing me naked, smoking in her bed after sex? Does it even matter?

When all's said and done.

Charlie

There's nowt quite like a blow job after school to relax your mind and help you think. Even if it is in a stinking cubicle in the boys' bogs.

Exams are next week. I've been revising but I'm finding it hard to focus. I never used to, but what with everything at home I just can't concentrate. It's the Mocks and all. I did OK, better than a lot of my teachers expected anyway, and now there's this pressure all of a sudden, not just for me to do well but for me to stay on and do A-Levels.

There's fuck all pressure coming from my dad, mind. Doing A-Levels means not getting a job and not being able to pay summat towards bills at home. The way things are right now – Dad not working and Mum not being able to – I don't have a choice.

I need to find a way to make money, fast, but the only thing I can come up with means paying a visit to Powerhouse Gym. There's no way I can square that with my dad, though. If there's one thing he hates more than drug dealers, it's Asians.

There's a word for that, I think as I zip up, grabbing my bag to do one. Unlucky.

Hayley

It's gone five and I'm still going through bloody Seamus Heaney with Mr Mitchell. He thinks I should a be doing the Advanced paper, even though the exam's in less than a week. I'm not so sure. There's this one poem, called *Digging*, and Mr Mitchell is underlining every other word, saying the man is digging with his pen, like his dad used to dig as a farmer.

> *Between my finger and my thumb,*
> *The squat pen rests.*
> *I'll dig with it.*

Seriously, though, how can you dig with a pen? As if.

'Don't take everything so literally, Hayley,' Mr Mitchell says, smiling. 'That's your problem. Open your mind a little, and try to see the imagery.'

He walks from the black board and perches himself on my desk, turning the page in my Anthology. He's actually quite handsome, Mr Mitchell, 'specially from the side. The way he's sitting, his jeans have gone proper tight on his thighs, which are quite muscular, and I can see his bulge.

I start to feel weird as he reads from another poem, this time by Wordsworth. Then I realise Mr Mitchell's turning me on and I can't help it. I just burst out laughing.

'What's the matter, Hayley?' he says, turning to face me. 'You think the expression "I wandered lonely as a cloud" is funny?'

He's not mad and actually seems to think it *is* funny, 'cause he starts laughing as well.

'That's good,' he says, walking back to the black board. 'Try and see the humour in language, how versatile it is, and how the writer doesn't always intend it to be understood literally . . . '

As he says this I think of Jenny and that lot earlier. Mr Mitchell might let me sit the Advanced paper, but I'll never get it all in time. Perhaps there was another reason why he wanted me to come back here after school, on my own.

My mind starts racing and I think of the way he thanked me, smiling all sheepish. I'm doing the Foundation for a reason – he must know that – and I'm no way brainy enough to be in the top set.

But I'm not stupid. After all, you shouldn't take everything so literally – isn't that what he just said?

With his back to me, I quickly reach under the desk, lift my skirt and slide my knickers down my legs. It's only after I've done this and slipped them into my blazer pocket, I remember I'm on the last day of my period. No wonder I'm so horny.

'Right, that should do it for today I think,' he says, turning to face me while standing at the board. 'We still have nearly a week before the exam, so if you think it *has* been useful please feel free to come after school again on Monday . . . '

He smiles that sheepish smile at me again, and I have a brainwave. As I pack my bag I see he's left a pile of old exam papers – the ones I helped him with earlier – on his desk. I make my way towards the door then turn back, as if forgetting summat.

'I, erm . . . forgot about those papers,' I say. 'Is it still OK for me to have one?'

'Of course . . . '

I can feel him watching me as I walk past. I get to the desk and in one movement, without making it look obvious, manage to accidentally-on-purpose knock the papers on the floor.

'Oops!' I say, trying to sound sexy, how Jenny Catlow would say it. 'I'll get them . . . ' I bend over slowly, my skirt already rolled up three times on my waist, and I can feel cold air on my bum and peach.

If Jenny Catlow could see me now.

CHAPTER FIVE

Russell

It's late by the time I get up the courage to leave, but as I approach the main doors I can see that I'm locked in. After pulling on the handle, I decide that my only hope is the fire escape at the end of the far corridor, across on the other side of school.

The place is always so quiet at this time but, as I get to the corridor, I see the lights on in Mr Mitchell's room. I stop, not wanting to bump into him. I was supposed to be going to one of his cramming sessions, but I haven't done the homework.

He asked me to write an essay on the person who meant the most to me – alive or dead. I've been writing you letters every week since you went away, but I didn't really want to hand one in. They're not meant for anyone but you.

I edge forwards and realise that his door is closed. If I'm quiet I can just slip right past, but as I tip-toe along a girl bursts out, practically in tears. It's Hayley. She doesn't notice me, just rushes down the fire escape, then Mr Mitchell comes out next but he sees me standing in the hall, and this seems to stop him from going after her.

'Sir,' I say, nodding.

I feel relieved. It looks a bit dodgy, and it's not as if he's going to bring up his cramming session now is it.

'Hello Russell,' he says sheepishly. 'You know . . . exam worries and, well . . . '

'Time of the month?' I say, immediately regretting it. I look out of the window and see Hayley running across the grass.

'Yes . . . erm . . . ' he stutters as I start to go after her. 'Time of the month indeed . . . '

Charlie

We come out of Maccy D's, jump the railings outside Poundland and see the bus at its stop. Brooker and Digger start sprinting but I can see people waiting and not getting on – there's no driver yet – so I take my time, strolling along past Kwik Save, the sign all smashed to bits, and eat my chips out the bag.

When I get to the stop, I stuff two cheeseburgers in my bag and stand at the back of the queue. Brooker and Digger are throwing chips about, but they pack it in when the driver turns up. He's got a skinhead and a diamond stud earring – looks hard, for a bus driver.

As I'm waiting to get on I make eye contact with this weird-looking threesome by the glass doors, not in the queue. The first one's an old gimmer. He looks pissed and seems to be scowling at me, but I can't tell. I think he's only got one eye. He's definitely pissed, though. I can smell him at ten paces. The other two with him are a couple, I reckon. The bloke's short and stocky. He's got two bulging carrier bags from JJB in each hand. They look old, like he's been using them for ages. His lanky bird's wearing stonewash blue jeans with creases ironed in the front, and black boots with a buckle on the ankles. She's like the cheapest slag you can think of. Her eyes are sunk, with dark circles underneath. She's missing some teeth and all. It's only when the bloke starts snogging her against the lamppost, after a bit, I look away.

I get home and almost trip over my mum in the kitchen. She's on her hands and knees, scrubbing the floor.

'Mum I already cleaned it.'

I crouch down so she can see me – her eyes aren't so good – but then there's a shout from the front room and she goes back to scrubbing.

'Charlie!' my dad shouts again. 'Don't meck me say it a third time, lad. Stop oinin' yer mum and come in 'ere.' I put the oven on gas mark six for tea and get my arse in the front room. It won't do to make him wait.

My dad's sprawled on the settee, an empty tumbler in his hands and a bottle of Bell's at his feet. He looks like he's been out. It's not Giro day, and he won't have bothered going down the job centre. He lost his job three years ago – got let go, to be exact – but what with the way things are he's not been able to get a new one. I see the paper rolled up, wedged down the side of his belly and the settee. He'll have been to the bookies. Yeah, that's it. He's back now 'cause it's closed.

'What d'you want for your tea, Dad?' I ask, struggling to hear myself over the telly, which is proper blaring. I know I'll be in trouble, 'cause it's a bit late for tea now and he'll want it before going back to the pub. 'I got some pizzas in – '

'Where've yer been?' he interrupts. 'It's gone six . . . '

'I just went into town after school, wi' Brooker and Digger.'

32

'Sound lads, them. Sound as a pound . . . ' He trails off and goes for the bottle on the floor, but he can't reach it. He sits on his arse all week, so it's no surprise he's a fat bastard.

I get it for him, then sit back down by the window.

'They 'ate us, Pakis. Understand lad?' He looks at me and I nod, before looking down at my feet. 'They 'ate us. So we 'ave t' 'ate 'em back . . . '

He stops talking and we sit in silence for a bit. I stare at the screen but it's been ages since I watched *Neighbours* and I don't recognise any of the characters. Then Dad changes channel in time for *North West Tonight*. The main story's about a body that's been found in a lay-by, round 'ere actually, with no head. It sounds hardcore so I try to listen in.

'Yer been at this?' he asks. I look away from the telly and he's staring at me, waving the bottle round. 'I 'ad a full bottle yesterday . . . '

'No Dad, I promise. I don't even like whisky . . . ' I get up to go and put the pizza in, but he grabs my arm as I pass the settee.

'Yer remember what I told yer, 'bout liars?' he says, gripping me. He might be a fat fucker but he's strong, make no mistake about it.

'I know,' I answer, making sure to look him in the eye. 'I'm not lyin' . . . '

'Good lad,' he says, letting go. 'Now go meck us some tea, eh? I'm off out in an 'our.'

I go in the kitchen and drink some water from the tap. Mum's still scrubbing the floor and I watch her for a bit then look away, out the window, at kids playing in the back street.

My phone vibrates in my pocket and I see I've got a text from Jenny:

R U doin owt 2nite? xXxXx

I look at my mum on the floor again. The oven beeps and I put the frozen pizza in, setting the timer for eighteen minutes.

I text her back:

Fuck all. Canal @ 9. Bring booze.

Hayley

I'm desperate for a wee so nip into McDonald's on my way home. I should've gone at school, but I was too embarrassed and couldn't face staying in that place for one more minute.

I cry a bit when I get into the cubicle, then I start laughing, mainly at how silly I'm being but also 'cause changing my tampon in McDonald's, on the last day of my period, reminds me of when I got my first.

I was with Mum, just before she died. I went to the loo and there was all this blood in my knickers.

'Mum,' I said, sticking my head round the door. The dryer was on and she didn't hear me. 'Mum!' I yelled, louder, just as the dryer stopped. I went really red. Red like my knickers.

'Why are you shouting, love?' she said, calm, and looking at me in the mirror.

'I think . . . well . . . there's blood in my knickers.' There was no other way of putting it.

34

'I have just the thing!' she said, chuckling.

Sitting here again in a McDonald's cubicle, putting a new tampon between my legs, makes me think of the time my mum, dying of cancer, slipped a ciggy under the door when I got my first period. You have to laugh.

On my way out of McDonald's I see Charlie. He's with Brooker and Digger, but they run off when they see the bus at its stop. There's no driver, though, so Charlie just wanders along, eating his chips.

I follow him, not too close, and think of what it would be like to walk past Kwik Save holding his hand, like we were going out. He wouldn't say owt – he's quiet really, y'know, the brooding type – but we'd be happy, just walking along holding hands.

Maybe we'd get a DVD and stay in at mine, curled up in front of the telly, all snugly and warm under my quilt. Then maybe we'd get bored of the DVD and start doing naughty stuff under it. I bet Charlie's amazing, under a quilt, and I can't think of anyone I'd rather lose my virginity to.

No, Charlie would be the best.

CHAPTER SIX

Russell

I texted Hayley. It seemed like a good idea at the time.

After I saw her running away from Mr Mitchell, I tried to catch up. It was only when I got halfway down the fire escape that I stopped, realising she probably has no idea who I am – or at best thinks I'm weird. My mind went blank, and I couldn't think of anything to say.

Then, when I was waiting in the bus station to change later, I saw two lads from school, Brooker and Digger. They got on my bus so I ducked behind a pillar and waited for the next one. I didn't want a repeat of this morning. My pants had only just dried out properly.

I crept out from behind the pillar and saw Hayley, waiting for the same bus as me. I couldn't believe it. She just sat down on one of the benches by the glass doors, got out her phone and started texting someone. There I was, only a few metres away from her. This, as they say, was my chance.

My legs wobbling, butterflies in my stomach, I started to walk in the direction of her bench – but then I hesitated. I was thinking, with every step, just a few more and I'll be sitting next to her.

Like before, though, I couldn't think of an opening line, so I veered off to my right and sat on a different bench.

I'd chickened out, again, but I'd also come up with a plan B. Watching her as she texted away and, without

36

making it look obvious, I pulled out my phone, considered what I wanted to say then settled, finally, on:

Are you OK?

I'd already sent it by the time I realised, I'd not even said who it was from.

Charlie

Brooker said he saw a body by the side of the canal and it might have no head, like that bloke they found, but he couldn't tell.

We're in the park and I don't know what I'm doing here. I came out to get away from it all, but I also wanted to talk to Jenny. I'm off my head now, though, so that's not going to happen. I just keep drinking 'cause there's more booze. Always more booze.

Brooker and Digger are messing round on the monkey bars, and I start thinking about these people I saw on the bus earlier. Four old codgers, craggy-faced, with long grey hair and baseball hats, tattoos on their arms, dressed like it was still the 1970s.

My dad once told me when you get out of prison you've changed inside but not out, 'cause you're dressed in the clothes you went in with. He spent some time inside a few years back, but I didn't really think about what he'd said until I saw those people on the bus.

'If I went to prison, tomorrow, I'd be dressed in a white shirt, blue jeans and a knackered pair of cherry Rockports,' I say, feeling pissed.

'Yer what Charlie?' Brooker shouts. He starts laughing. 'Oi Digger, Charlie's well out of it!'

'Yer reet Charlie?' Jenny's now by my side, her arm round my waist.

'Yeah yeah,' I say, straightening up. 'Pass me that . . . ' I point at the bottle of vodka she's holding.

'Kiss me and I'll give it yer.'

I grab her by the waist, proper tight, like the way my dad gripped me earlier. She looks scared, but then I grin and kiss her hard on the mouth.

I must be really pissed, 'cause the next thing I know she's sucking me off on the swings. I can't see owt else – it's dark and there are no lights in the park – but I can hear Brooker and Digger arguing.

'*You* do it then if yer so 'ard,' says one of them.

'Yer the one actin' like yer' fuckin' business,' says the other.

I get off the swings, pull my jeans up, then stagger over to see what they're on about.

'What's goin' off?'

'Brooker dared us to go back and see if that body were still there,' Digger says, 'and I told 'im there's no fuckin' way I'm goin' up there on me own.'

'Pussy . . . ' Brooker mutters.

'*You* go then!' Digger looks like he's about to cry, clenching his fists. He's always been scared of Brooker, even though he's twice his size. I suppose that says a lot about Brooker.

'Calm down. We'll all go, alreet?'

On our way, Jenny holding on to me, we pass this black prozzer standing all alone by a smashed up bus stop. I've never seen any black people round 'ere, so she stands out for that reason anyway, but she's wearing a dress that's too short for her and when she turns round, to offer her wares, you can see her arse.

'I'll give yer a tenner if yer ask for a blow job, Digs,' says Brooker.

'Alreet then,' he answers, starting to cross the street.

'Stop fuckin' about,' I say, giving him a dig to the shoulder. 'Are we goin' canal or not?'

'Soz Charlie,' he says, holding his shoulder. 'I was only messin' about . . . '

When we get to the canal some lads I don't recognise, about our age, are hanging round the ditch where Brooker said he saw the body. There are four of them, but before I can say owt Brooker and Digger are spoiling for a fight.

'Oi oi what's this?' Digger shouts. 'Get away from our mate!' They start running towards the lads and have both taken out weapons – Brooker a blade, Digger his Stanley knife.

'Yer want some?' Brooker yells, squaring up to the biggest one, which is the best thing to do. The others run away, predictable little fuckers, leaving him to face Brooker and Digger, who by now are both laughing.

When me and Jenny catch up we can see the body still lying in the ditch. There's no movement, but it's too dark to see if it's got a head or not.

'There, there,' Brooker carries on, putting his arm round the lad. 'Don't worry, we're not gonna hurt yer . . . ' Digger kneels down behind the lad and Brooker shoves him over, then gets on top of him and holds the blade to his throat.

'Let's go,' Jenny whispers. My head's spinning and I don't want to be here either. She starts pulling on me. 'Come on Charlie. Let's leave 'em to it . . . '

'Why d'yer always leave before the fun starts, Jen?' says Brooker, still kneeling on the lad, who looks like he's about to shit himself. 'Yer no fun . . . '

'Leave it Brook,' I say. 'It's not worth – '

'I don't give a shit about 'im,' Jenny interrupts. 'Do what yer want . . . slash 'is face for all I care!'

I've never seen her like this before. She's proper animated and shouting, probably 'cause of the pills we did earlier. I'm in a daze and starting to think they were duff.

'Prove it then,' says Digger, walking over to us.

'What d'yer mean?' she says. 'Want me to cut this lad?'

'Nah . . . I want yer to set fire t' body.' He pulls a lighter from his pocket and holds it out with a bottle of vodka. Brooker's laughing his head off and the lad starts crying, realising he's probably next.

'Jenny . . . ' I say, taking her hand. I look over at the body in the ditch. It's still not moving.

'Alreet then,' she says, ignoring me and pushing my hand away. 'Nowt like a bit of madness on a Friday night, eh?'

I'm about to try and stop her, but I feel too pissed and instead just stand there, rooted to the spot, as she empties the bottle of vodka over the body. She's in hysterics, jumping round and shrieking, and my head's now thumping, like someone's proper smacking me over and over again in the side of the face and won't fucking stop. I try to focus on the body, come to my senses, but

Brooker and Digger just keep egging her on, goading her to set it on fire.

'Do it Jen do it do it!' they both keep shouting, like they're the same person or summat.

And what's funny is, the body doesn't move an inch, doesn't even flinch, as Jenny, looking me in the eye now, drops the lighter.

Everyone jumps back 'cause of this sudden explosion of fire around us, a massive flame that lights up the whole fucking mess. And even though I'm too pissed to care, I can see it all. I can see everything.

The body has no head.

Hayley

I hate staying in on a Friday night, but I have no money so am watching DVDs with Gemma and Laura and all wrapped up in my quilt. I'm nice and warm but, well, it's not exactly what I had in mind.

'Did you watch *Britain's Got Talent* earlier?' Laura asks, as soon as the film finishes.

'I didn't know it was on,' I answer.

I'm not really interested to tell the truth. Instead, I'm thinking about what Charlie's doing right now. I bet he's doing summat cool. Maybe he went up the canal, or into town. I'd have gone, if I had any money, but Dad said I'd already gone out enough this month and needed to revise.

'Yeah *Hayley,* it's the auditions,' says Gemma, giving me a dirty look like I should've known that. 'I can't believe that one what looks like Amy Winehouse got through.'

'The only one what shocked me was that twenny-six

41

year old. Y'know, the weird looking one . . . '

'I don't know what you're goin' on about,' I say, fed up.

'She has proper thin eyebrows and, like, a big forehead? Y'know . . . '

'The one who looks like a chink?' says Gemma.

There's a pause, and Laura looks like she's thinking proper hard about it.

'Yeah, that's her.'

I yawn and start to think about going to bed. Then I see my phone flashing, grabbing it before Laura can.

'I'm goin' t' loo,' I say, already halfway out the room.

I lock the door and sit down on the side of the bath. There's one unread message, but it's from a few hours ago. I've had it on silent since earlier, when I was at Mr Mitchell's thing. I don't recognise the number, though, and it just says:

Are you OK?

I start racking my brains to think who it might be from. I've had this same number for yonks 'cause Dad won't buy me a new phone. I keep asking for one for Christmas, but he just says I'm fine with the one I've got.

I think again. I know who I'd like it to be from, but I don't think Charlie has my number. I wish. It could be a wrong number I suppose but, then again, what if it's not? What if it's from someone I've just met?

Someone like, Mr Mitchell?

CHAPTER SEVEN

Russell

'Why aren't you at school?' my mum asks, startling me.
She's in default position, slumped in her armchair by the
window, a cigarette in her mouth, the ashtray on the arm.
From where she's sitting, next to the net curtains, she can
watch telly and the neighbours at the same time.

'It's Saturday, Mum,' I answer, putting on my new
Doc Martens. I've got a part-time packing job at a
factory, but it's taken me ages to save up for them.
'Otherwise,' I continue, under my breath, 'you wouldn't
be able to sit on your bum watching bloody James
Martin, would you?'

She doesn't seem to care whether I'm talking or not,
though. She's just staring out of the window.

'Bye Mum,' I say, hovering in the doorway. Still no
response. I could take these boots off and throw them at
her, and she still wouldn't notice me.

I'm going to see my cousin Jason in Leeds today. I'm
staying tonight too, which will be good. I have to wait at
Manchester Road station, though, because I mistimed it
and caught the early bus. There are some younger boys
waiting under the shelter, messing around, so I walk to
the other end of the platform, in case they start on me.

After standing there for half an hour, I get on the train,
which is an old one with seats that expel dust when you sit
down. I pick up a paper and start reading about a headless

body that's been found. The police haven't been able to identify it yet, apparently, but they think it's drugs-related. It seems everything's drugs-related round here, though. Sometimes I think that I'm the only kid in the world who's not off his head.

When I was eleven my mum ran away from home – do you remember? It was around the time she stopped working and started taking stuff, just to get through the day. She left on a Friday and came back on the Monday, in the end, but we were on our own all weekend. We raided the drinks cabinet and downed a bottle of Bailey's. I woke up in the bath the next day. It was enough to put me off for life.

I put my headphones in and listen to Bowie all the way to Bradford Interchange. My MP3 player is one of those pen drive types. The battery in it only lasts a few hours – I've brought four as back up – and the USB plug bit is bent and exposed because I lost the top. I only got it last Christmas but Jason told me he'd buy me an iPod for my birthday, so hopefully I'll not have to put up with it for much longer.

Bradford's a dump. You have to come out of the station the way you come in, but in reverse, so you get to enjoy the panoramic views across the town twice. In case you missed anything the first time around.

I change track to something Jason told me to download. I've always been into older music really, but this band's called Performance and, I don't know, they're just really different. I've been listening to them quite a bit actually. There's this one part that repeats, and it makes me want to write songs.

It's foolish to belong. You knew it all along.

The song stops and I look out of the window. We're pulling into Leeds. Two identical tower blocks, Clyde Court and Clyde Grange, are situated not far from some amazing glass apartments, the kind that they build for yuppies. Imagine looking out of your window, maybe having breakfast on the balcony, and being able to see these ugly tower blocks full of poor people. I bet they don't like it at all.

The train sits there for a while before eventually pulling into Leeds station. I take out my directions – Jason texted me them last night, but I wanted to write them down, just in case – then make my way to a hotel bar in the city centre.

It's all glass and shiny and loud colours, and I feel a bit silly wandering through the lobby, groups of posh people in suits looking at me in my scruffy clothes and Doc Martens, but then I find the bar Jason told me about and sit down away from everyone, by the window.

I'm about an hour early, but nobody bothers me. I just sit staring out of the window at a mesmerising billboard across the street. It's huge, flashes of blue and white, yellow and red, images of clothes and jewellery and, for some reason, discount train tickets. *Lifestyle*, I think. That's what it's all about.

Strange music is playing in the bar, flutes and sitars, and this girl singing in French. It's new to me, this hotel music. Come to think of it, I don't think that I've ever been in a hotel bar before. Not like this anyway.

When I was little we used to go to Blackpool. I called it 'Cesspool' – well, behind Mum's back. Mum was working

45

then but, still, we never stayed anywhere nice like this. It was always Bed and Breakfasts full of old fogies.

I don't like it in this bar, not really, but Jason wanted to meet here. He said that he works nearby and comes here quite a lot. He also said that the food's good, Japanese I think, and I should try a virgin cocktail. I've already seen them on the suede menu and, even though a drink called 'virgin' is appropriate for me, I'm sticking with Coke all the same.

Bang! There's a slam against the window, startling me. It's Jason, standing at the glass and waving. He glides away, presumably to the door, and I feel myself going red. It's as if everyone's looking at me.

A moment later, he appears across the bar, motioning for a waiter to follow him to the table where I'm sitting, embarrassed. He looks cool in baggy jeans and trainers, and he's also wearing sunglasses but takes them off as he gets to my table. I stand up, not sure whether to shake his hand, but he just gives me a big hug.

'How are you little fella?' he says, smiling widely as he pulls away, looking me up and down. 'You look good.'

I don't. My hair's a mess and I'm really spotty today. I tried to cover them with Mum's concealer but it's the wrong colour, too orange, and they probably look worse now.

'Hi . . . ' I manage, not sure what to say. 'You look . . . nice, I mean . . . ' I trail off. Jason always makes me nervous, even though he's the sweetest person in the world. The only sweet person I know, in fact. 'I mean, you look – '

'Cool . . . ?' he interrupts, smiling. 'Thought not!' He

laughs and we sit down. He squeezes my thigh. 'Are you hungry? Let's eat.'

'I haven't got any . . . ' I say, trailing off again. 'I mean, Mum didn't have any money and I only have about a tenner . . . from the factory. I normally work Saturdays but saved it from last weekend, erm . . . ' I present the now crumpled ten pound note, as if Jason's never seen one before.

'Don't be a numpty all your life,' he says, grinning and putting his arm around me. 'Two cheeseburgers please,' he says to a passing waitress. 'Is that OK?' he adds, to me.

'Erm . . . yes . . . thanks.'

'Cool,' he says, handing the menus back to her. 'Thank you.'

Jason's a graphic designer and lives in a flat like the ones I saw from the train. He's my cousin on Dad's side of the family, and the only person on that side who stays in touch. I think it's to make up for the fact that Dad's gone – you know, to make sure we're alright and don't throw ourselves off the multi-storey car park.

He thinks I should apply to Leeds, after I've done my A-Levels, and says I could even stay with him. I don't know whether he means it or feels like he has to offer. We can't afford the fees and Mum thinks that loans are a bad idea, even though she's got more than a few herself. I want to do a course in creative writing, but she says it's not a proper subject, so I don't really know.

I just want to escape. Seeing Jason is great because, well, it makes it easier to forget that I probably never will.

Charlie

I don't know whether it was Friday night, when Jenny went mental, or just now, when Brooker and Digger told me they stole some lad's Doc Martens and chucked them in the canal, but I'm fucked off.

I can't be arsed with drinking all the time and sitting round 'ere doing nowt, I can't be arsed with Brooker and Digger, and I definitely can't be arsed with Jenny. She thinks we're going out, but we're not. I told her just now by the canal and she got upset, but I just walked off and left them to it.

Fuck it. It's still weekend and the world's my oyster. I take out my phone and check the time, thinking about where to go and what to do on a Sunday afternoon, then realising there's fuck all to do round 'ere any day of the week.

I decide to take Ish up on his offer and go see him at Powerhouse Gym. I need to come up with a way to make money somehow, and it can't hurt to find out what's what.

In the station there's this girl from school, Hayley, waiting for the same bus. She avoids making eye contact with me, probably 'cause she reckons I'm thick as pig shit and a troublemaker, which is fair enough I suppose. It only takes about ten minutes to get across town 'cause the trendy driver from the other day puts his foot down. I reckon he's sound, that bloke. Hayley's still on when I get off, but she doesn't see me when I look up at the window 'cause she's on her phone.

The whole area, near Powerhouse Gym, is Asian. There's this little lad, and he stares at me as I walk past the Co-op.

I feel a vibe and want to tell him, even though he's a Muslim, it's OK.

I walk on, passing a woman dressed in all black head to toe, so you can't see owt apart from her eyes. She's wearing glasses and all, so even then you can't make out her features. I smile but then think better of it, and look down at my feet instead.

I feel a bit self-conscious waltzing up there, but I make eye contact with the Asians hanging round their BMWs outside so they know I mean business, even though I'm actually brickin' it.

I walk in, then downstairs. It stinks of sweat and summat else I can't place – powdery but also sickly sweet. Ish is talking to two lads by the free weights. They've got big arms and shoulders but big bellies and all. I expected everyone to have good bodies and that, but I don't think much of what's on show to be honest.

'These lot fucked this fuckin' junky up proper good style,' Ish is saying, laughing. 'The bird's a junky and all, so they used 'er to get to 'im, settin' up a meetin', like, at 'er flat – '

'Honeypot,' one of the lads interrupts. 'I've seen it on that programme about gangs, that one wi' Danny Dyer . . . '

'Yeah yeah 'oneypot, that's it,' says Ish. 'And so anyway . . . yer've made me forget what I were sayin'!' He punches the lad on his arm, hard but just messing. 'Oh yeah, when 'e turned up, expecting to see 'er, maybe smoke some, maybe get 'is end away, they did 'im. One of 'em 'eld 'im while the other stabbed 'im 'bout twenny times. Then – and this is the *proper sick* part – they set it up like it were 'er what did it.' Ish breaks off, laughing. 'See, they got this 'arness,

49

this proper fuckin' sick swing or summat, like the ones pervs 'ave, and they stripped the junky and strapped 'im in. The pigs found 'im like that, wi' 'is bird passed out in t' other room. And *she* got done for it! Alreet Charlie lad?'

Ish has turned round, taking me by surprise.

'Glad yer could make it. It's good to see yer. Waj is gettin' changed but 'ang round and we'll go somewhere a bit quieter.' He holds out his hand and I shake it, his long, thick fingers full of rings made of Asian gold – more yellow than gold, and proper chunky.

'What's that smell?' I ask. I'm not sure why. It's the first thing that came into my head.

'That's exactly what I said when I first cem 'ere!' one of the lads answers, laughing. The two of them both shake my hand. For some reason all the Asians are obsessed with it – fuck knows why.

'It's protein shake,' says Ish, smiling. 'Powerhouse branded. Yer want one?'

'Fuck no!' I say, laughing, but everyone's gone quiet all of a sudden.

I turn round and see this older Asian lad standing by the door, staring at me. He's wearing all black, his hair wet. The others have it shaved close but his is long, slicked back. He's only wearing a vest on top, showing off a big fuck off pair of biceps, and you can tell they're shit scared of him, just from their reactions. They don't even look at him, and all go back to doing whatever the fuck they were doing before.

'Charlie lad,' Ish says, handing him a leather jacket, 'this is Waj . . . '

I'm about to shake his hand, but he just ignores me and walks out, Ish following on. I stand there for a bit, looking like a spare part.

'I'd get goin' if I were you,' one of the lads says, smiling.

I go outside, sharpish, and see Waj climb into his X5. Ish motions for me to get in the back, and we drive off.

There's silence, until Waj puts on some music. I recognise the song but there's so much bass I can't make out the lyrics. Waj keeps looking at me in the rear-view mirror, and I see he has bright blue contact lenses in.

'You're not scared are you?' he says, his voice flat, chilled out. I realise straight away he's not from round 'ere. I was expecting him to sound rough but he's proper well-spoken, no accent or owt.

I think about the question for a sec, then answer.

'Nah. Should I be?'

Ish laughs, then I catch a bit of the song.

> *Stop scheming, and looking hard,*
> *I got a great big bodyguard.*

'I like the look of you,' says Waj, turning the music down and looking at me in the mirror. 'I think we'll make a good team.' He turns the volume up again.

> *I get money, money I got . . .*

Most shops in town are closed on a Sunday, but Originals is always open. Waj parks in front of the shop and I follow as the two of them make their way inside.

'I'll take those in a size eleven,' says Waj, grabbing some Paul Smith shoes from the window as soon as he gets in the shop, and gesturing to a blonde girl standing behind the till. 'That jumper,' he carries on, snatching a Paul &

51

Shark cardigan from a display, 'these shirts . . . and this jacket.' He piles two Hugo Boss shirts, really crisp, and a Barbour jacket on the counter.

The shop assistant's gobsmacked, like she's not seen owt like it before. I know how she feels.

'Don't yer wanna try 'em on or owt?' she asks.

'No,' he says, deadpan. 'I know my size.'

She takes out a calculator and starts reckoning up. It seems to take forever, like she's never used one before. 'That'll be . . . erm . . . £1,100 . . . please . . . ' she says, embarrassed.

Waj takes a huge wad of notes from his jacket pocket and counts out, in fifties, the exact amount. The dizzy blonde just stares at him as he piles up the cash in front of her, then walks out the shop, leaving Ish to carry the bags. I follow them both out, not knowing what to think. I've never seen that much cash in my life.

We drive across town, me in the back, the music blaring. Then Waj pulls up to some black gates and a block of apartments. He tells me he owns the penthouse as we get into a lift, but the lounge has barely any furniture, just two plasma screens and a big black leather settee. He shows me round and these screens are everywhere – in the kitchen, even one in the bathroom.

I didn't notice at first, but there's also this young Chinese-looking girl lying on that settee in the lounge. I couldn't see her from behind it – that's how big it is. She's naked, and I must look surprised 'cause she giggles, before getting up and going off to the bedroom. She looks younger than me and Ish, and Waj clocks me watching her.

'Don't worry about her, Charlie. I brought her back from Bangkok. She cleans and she fucks.' I just nod, not really understanding how that works. 'I might take you one day, if you're lucky. We do a lot of business there. And if you have money, you can buy anything – '

'Why am I here again?' I interrupt. As I say this, Ish starts laughing.

'I said Charlie's funny din-I?' he says. 'Dunt give a shit!'

'OK Charlie,' says Waj, standing in front of one of the plasmas, watching me close. 'I won't waste your time. I want you to deal to gora – first at school, to start you off, then at other schools, then the rest of town. Understand?'

'Why can't you deal to whites?' I ask, trying to make eye contact but not come across fly.

'Because you won't buy from *Pakis*. Unless it's a pint of milk, or a chicken tikka masala.' Ish laughs but Waj's face doesn't change. He just lights a fag, then looks me up and down. 'You, Charlie, are going to help me change that.'

'By selling drugs for you?'

'By selling *product* for me.' He walks past where I'm standing and sits down on the settee, next to Ish. 'I'm a businessman, Charlie, and right now the white gangs are stealing my business. I have a monopoly on the Asians, but now I want the same for gora . . . ' He takes a long drag, then looks back at me. 'We're at war.'

I think about that headless bloke they found when he says this last part. The police don't know jack shit, as per, but it's all about territory. Always is.

'You in Charlie lad?' says Ish, snapping me out of it.

I knew they'd want me to push drugs, and I wasn't all

that keen when Ish talked to me last week. Now Waj has just said he's at war, I'm even less keen.

I must give this away 'cause Waj comes over and puts his arm round me.

'Look at this, Charlie,' he says, taking the wad of notes from his jacket pocket. 'You saw me in Originals. I bring in more money than I know what to do with. So does everyone who works for me. The only problem is, *spending it.*'

Waj leads me over to the balcony, gripping me by the neck, hard enough for me to understand he's not fucking about. I can see his X5 in the car park down below. It's high up, and I start to regret interrupting him earlier.

'You've got your exams soon?' he carries on, his eyes focused on mine. I nod. 'You join me and you'll not need to worry about school ever again.'

'You in Charlie lad?' asks Ish, again.

I don't say owt, then Waj hands me some notes.

'That's yours,' he says, letting go of my neck then smiling. 'Just for turning up today. No strings attached.'

I count it. There's £250. I think about my dad, and how much money I'd be earning if I left school and got a proper job. Then I think about how much money I could be earning with this lot, no matter if I stayed on next year or not.

'I was gonna get a job packin' in a factory or summat,' I say, 'over summer . . . '

Ish laughs.

'What does that pay?' Waj asks, raising an eyebrow.

'£3.51 an hour,' I reply, putting the notes in the back pocket of my jeans, then smiling. 'Fuck it. I'm in.'

Hayley

I'm in McDonald's again listening to Gemma going on about summat or other, bless her, and slurping at the dregs of a chocolate milkshake. It tastes funny, like they've not put enough syrup in, but I can't be bothered to take it back and ask for another.

'He's bipolar,' she's saying. 'I didn't know, though. I just thought he didn't like me . . . '

'I think I'm gonna go home,' I say, licking my straw.

'Yeah I'm bored and all,' she says. 'Shall we watch a DVD? I've got that weird one wi' Jared Leto. It's about druggies or summat – '

'Well actually,' I interrupt, 'I think I'm just gonna get in, do some revisin' then get to bed early.' I start feeling bad as soon as her little face drops, so desperately try and think of summat nice to say. 'See ya tomorrow?' is all I can manage, though.

I leave McDonald's and walk to the bus station, passing Poundland and Sidewalk, which always used to be proper rammed but is now boarded up, then Planet Chicken, where everyone goes after a night out. It's not got anyone in now but I can still smell the greasiness. It's enough to make you a veggie, but I couldn't do that. Dad wouldn't let me.

Wandering into the station, I start to think about him. He should be in when I get back. It *is* Saturday night, after all. That's why I left really, 'cause I'd like to spend some time with him. We used to do stuff always. We'd go shopping, or on the Turf, or we'd just walk round Towneley and he'd buy me a 99.

I stop daydreaming when I see Charlie getting on the

same bus. He sees me and I look away, feeling myself going red, but I need to get home so I go to the back of the queue. I daren't look at him, so just stare at my feet or pretend to text people. When he gets off, I talk into my phone so he doesn't catch me looking.

While I'm doing this, I think about how funny it would be if my phone suddenly went off, and the other people on the bus realised I was pretending. It doesn't, but it would've been funny if it had.

I get home and Dad's lying on the settee.

'Sweet 'eart . . . ' he says, starting to get up.

'No don't, Dad,' I say, going over and giving him a big hug. 'Stay where you are.'

'I Sky-plussed that programme you like,' he says, sitting back again. 'Fancy watchin' it wi' us?'

'I'll make us a brew.'

I get changed into my jim-jams while the kettle's boiling, and bring my quilt down so we can be nice and close, like I used to with Mum. Then we watch telly without saying a word, until it goes off.

'The sad thing is it 'appens,' he says. 'It's like that poor bloke wi' no 'ead. Y'know they think that's drugs and all now? They said it on t' news earlier. It's everywhere . . . '

It was about gangs, the programme, but nowt like how it really is – y'know, typical BBC with all these posh folk pretending to be from places like round 'ere. I only watch it 'cause I know Dad likes that kind of thing.

'How was work?' I ask, changing the subject, then wishing I hadn't.

'Y'know 'ow it is sweet 'eart,' he says, ready to go off on

56

one. 'It's a tuppence apney business, and they're cutting everyone's hours back. I'm good at sod all unless it's wi' me 'ands. But no bugger makes owt no more . . . 'ave I taken yer round t' industrial estate lately?' I shake my head. 'It's all wholesalers, finishers. There used to be a steel industry a few miles from 'ere. Now it's a shopping centre or summat, a bowling alley – '

'And a Frankie & Benny's,' I say, interrupting. 'It's nice food, though, Frankie & Benny's.' He smiles but I don't think he gets it, bless him.

'It's not just me. Nobody's got any brass round 'ere. Business 'as gone for a burton, but they talk about a credit crunch on t' news like it's summat new. Credit crunch? This town's been in recession for twenny years, and what's anyone done about it? Nowt. The place is on its arse . . . '

When I was on the bus earlier, I saw a sign next to a bit of land behind Asda. It said *Investing In Your Town* but the poster was ripped and peeling off, and it didn't look like owt was happening or even about to really. I think about telling him, but I don't want him to go on so change the subject again.

'Shall we watch a film?' I say, trying to sound excited. 'I'll make us some of that popcorn we got. It might be nice . . . ' I smile at him and he smiles back. 'How about a scary 'un? We can hide under my quilt!'

'Whatever yer want sweet 'eart.'

Even though he goes on about there being no jobs, I like it when we spend time together. At least he's here, not down the bookies like everyone else's dad.

And I love him for that.

CHAPTER EIGHT

Russell

Those two lads from school robbed my Doc Martens and gave me a black eye earlier, so now I'm lying on my bed, crying, while thinking about your breasts. I hope you're happy.

I was your first. Not your first in that way, obviously, but the first boy you showed your breasts to. You never let me forget it. And I haven't.

We were up at the rec, lying on our backs in the penalty area, hot and sweaty from running around and trying to play a match as the greatest ever Man U side. It was hard because, as the only outfield player, you had to be everyone in the team. Beckham on the halfway line, over to Giggs on the left wing, then run into position at the edge of the box, dribble around a few imaginary Chelsea players, square to Rooney then – smash! A twenty-yarder, right in the top corner.

Anyway, there we were on our backs in the penalty area, looking up at the clear blue sky and the trails left by distant planes high above us, on the way to somewhere else, somewhere exciting.

'Anywhere's more exciting than this shithole . . . ' you groaned.

You couldn't wait to grow up and leave, and always said that you just wanted to escape. Seeing those planes only made you long for it even more. But I think, like me, you didn't really want to be anywhere else. Not in that moment, lying there together, looking up at the clear blue sky.

'I'm so hot . . . ' I said.

'Take your top off then,' you said, not looking at me. 'I don't mind – '

'Take yours off!' I said – joking, I think.

And you did. You removed your sweaty T-shirt to reveal two faintly rounded but as yet undeveloped breasts, and two pink, puffy nipples.

'You've got a hardon!' you shouted, turning and looking down at the bulge in my shorts.

'Get lost!' I said, covering myself.

'Ooh, would you like to rub it against my tits? Ooh, spunk on my tits? Ooh yeah . . . ' You started touching them, messing around and acting like an idiot, as usual.

'Seriously, get lost . . . ' I said, getting up and storming off.

I don't know if you care, but I can already picture my first time with a girl.

There's a long corridor and a room with a discoloured door, a naked bulb swaying from a dusty cord. A young girl sits on a double bed, her legs crossed. She's thin with pale skin, big eyes and long blonde hair. She's smoking what smells like a joint but puts it out when I move closer. She doesn't look at me. When she does, she holds eye contact, removing her dress and reclining on the bed, which has no bedding, and opens her legs. She's shaved and looks sore. I climb on top of her and look into deep glassy eyes, large and open, always open. I close mine when I enter her, and don't open them until it's over.

And as we do this without feeling, I'll picture that time when you showed me your breasts. I won't be able to remember you, not properly, as you were in that beautiful moment we shared at the rec, when we were just eleven years old. That moment, as with all beautiful moments, is now lost. But it won't matter.

I'll still wish it was you there with me instead.

Charlie

'Alright' by Supergrass is on the radio, and I'm watching two kids dancing on the front step of a terraced house as we drive by in the X5. Waj puts in a new CD, but it was almost like they were dancing to the song in the car.

One of them looks about eleven, skinny with cropped blonde hair, dressed in tiny shorts. She keeps looking at me, sitting in the back of the X5 as we stop at the lights. I stare back, thinking it's only a matter of time before some boy from school, or maybe one who dropped out and went on the dole, picks her up in his Vauxhall Nova, takes her somewhere nice and quiet overlooking the shithole where they're both from, and pushes her into letting him slide one finger, then two, inside her tight, dry cunt.

The car drives on and Waj turns the music off, before parking in front of Genesis in town. It's quiet but two lads are loitering outside.

'OK Charlie, you know what to do,' he says, looking at me in the rear-view mirror. 'Just get them interested, then leave it to me.' I nod, to show him I understand. 'Lock

60

the car, and I'll see you upstairs.' He chucks me the keys then gets out with Ish, leaving me in the back.

I should be revising but Waj said he wants me to get started straight away, and I didn't want to argue with him. I get out and lock the car, before walking over to the lads.

'You got a light mate?' I ask, pulling out a joint and looking at the biggest one. He's stocky with a shaved head and a gold earring in his left ear, probably that Invincible Hoop from Elizabeth Duke, if I had to guess.

'Yeah mate,' he says, holding out a lighter. I take a long drag and blow the smoke to my right, not taking my eyes off him.

'You lads want owt?' I ask, passing the joint and lifting my chin, my eyes still locked on his.

'Nah mate,' he says, losing eye contact and looking down the street.

'You got any bag?' asks his mate, excited. He's got a skinhead and all but looks a proper weed, these shit tribal tattoos all over his scrawny arms.

'Not on me, no,' I answer, frowning so he knows I think he's a dickhead. 'D'you think I'd be here on my own wi' bag? What do I look like? A fuckin' Paki?'

The biggest one laughs then his mate does too, and I realise why Waj wants me on board. These two are both so thick they didn't even notice me getting out the same car as two Asians, not two minutes ago.

'You got the readies, though?' The scrawny one removes a wad of twenties from his pocket and I realise he's serious. 'Alreet then!' I say, smiling.

I lead the way into the club and they follow me upstairs

to the VIP, where Waj and Ish are sitting with Asif.

'Don't mind them,' I say, my voice low. 'They do the dirty work.' They both laugh again, like they're in on it. 'You fellas been here before?' I carry on, putting my arm round the biggest one, my back to his mate.

'Nah but it looks alreet – '

'These'll sort you out,' I interrupt, introducing them to Ish and Asif, who are now surrounded by a group of girls, all about my age, maybe younger.

I laugh and turn to face the two lads as they sit down and eye up the girls.

'Oi oi!' I shout, getting their attention by clapping my hands, then making sure Waj is watching. 'Nowt like a bit of madness on a Sunday night, eh?'

Hayley

'I'm not fat I'm curvy, so shut up!'

I'm on the phone to Gemma. I need to know what time our first exam is on Monday, but she's just going on and on about her new diet. She keeps telling me she wants to look like Laura, but she's so skinny she makes those size zero celebs in *Heat* look like chunky monkeys.

I drift off a bit, thinking about the time Gemma went on a diet last summer. When I told Dad, he just laughed.

'She'll be fat as long as she's an 'ole in 'er arse,' he said. 'Don't let it rub off on yer sweet 'eart. Yer gorgeous.'

I suddenly realise Gemma's still talking.

' . . . and she's started on those Nicorette Inhalator thingies, but Laura reckons she looks like she's smokin' a tampon – '

'Gemma! I need to know when our exam is. Y'know? On Monday?'

'Oh who cares?' she says, giggling. 'You're rubbish at Maths. Proper braindead, like me.'

That's true, but I still need to try. I need five Cs to get into Drama school, and I don't really know how I'll manage it. I'm rubbish at Maths, like Gemma says, but I don't think I'll get a C in History – too much essay writing and my hand always feels like it'll drop off when I have to write loads – or French – I'll mess up my Oral, deffo – so that just leaves Maths, Science, English Language, which I talk everyday so should be OK at really, and English Lit. You get two for Science, so that would be five. I suppose I'm not that bad at Maths after all.

'I'm gonna go t' bed Gems . . . '

'Happy revising . . . swot!'

I'm not tired, course, but instead of revising I end up flicking channels on the telly. The picture's rubbish and I think the freeview box Dad got me's knackered. ITV2's OK, though, so I watch the end of *I'm a Celebrity*, then there's an aftershave advert with this proper yummy bloke. He's got a well cut body and a face like a Disney Prince.

I check my phone but don't have any new messages. I haven't had anything else from that mystery number, but that's probably only 'cause I've not replied.

Smiling to myself, I slip it under the pillow then drift off into dreamland, thinking thoughts of living happily ever after with my Prince Charming, somewhere far, far away from here.

CHAPTER NINE

Russell

Seeing cows running in a field makes me think of you. I'm sorry. It just does.

To get to the rec, we had to cut across a farmer's field. Remember? I always carried the football and gave you a leg up over the barbed wire fence. I didn't mind, because it meant contact. And sometimes I'd get to look up your skirt. You didn't mind, because you liked it when I looked up your skirt. And you never mentioned it, which makes me smile, now, sitting here thinking of you on this bus to nowhere.

School, actually, but it might as well be nowhere.

We pull into the bus station and there's a change of driver. The new one, a butch-looking woman, starts talking to the Asian one who's taking forever to get off. They do this every day, and I start to worry that I'll be late for my first exam – especially when I see Brooker and Digger getting on. When they beat me up, the last time, they wrote *ME = FREAK* on my forehead in black marker.

I slide down in my seat, wishing the world would just swallow me up right here, and try to avoid making eye contact with them by burying my head in a *Citizen*. The headline is about another body being found in a ditch, up by the canal. It'd been set on fire and the body was missing a head, just like the one from before.

I look up, peering over the top of my newspaper, and

see Hayley. She's on her own, and looks nice with her hair up. I watch her as she approaches, hoping she'll sit down in the spare seat next to me.

Hayley's not like other girls our age. She's nothing like Jenny Catlow and all the popular girls, and I think she knows it. That's what makes her different, though. That's what makes her special.

She walks past me to the back of the bus, and I feel myself slumping even lower down in my seat – so low that I'm practically on the floor. When I dare to look around, though, I can see that she's still not found a seat. The only free ones are next to Brooker and Digger. She turns and sees me looking, then notices that the seat next to me is free. I try to act casual by turning to look out of the window, as she stands next to me, hesitates for what feels like two lifetimes, then sits down.

We travel for two stops before I find the courage to say anything.

'Hi . . . Hayley,' I manage, almost forgetting her name because I'm so nervous.

'Hi Russell,' she says, not looking at me.

'So erm . . . how's the revision going?' I can't think of anything else to say, so pick the most boring and unsexy topic imaginable. Sometimes I think that I should just write everything down and communicate with the aid of cue cards. That way, I'll never have to speak to anyone ever again.

'OK I suppose,' she says, looking in her bag for something.

There's a pause while I try and think of a follow up,

desperate for this moment to last, and desperate not to mess it up.

'I was thinking of going to Mr Mitchell's thing . . . you know . . . but I really couldn't be bothered. I must have read that poem a million times now. I get it. He's just like his dad . . . ' I force a laugh.

She turns around, and looks right at me. 'Yeah I don't usually like poetry, but I quite like that actually. You should give it another go.' She smiles to herself and takes out her phone.

I never did get a reply from her. I'm not surprised and can't even be sure that she got the message. The phone she's holding now doesn't look new, but I doubt she's had the same one since Year Seven. Even I've had a new one since then, and my mum hasn't worked in years.

I look out of the window, and smile. Not only did she notice me, but we had a real life connection. And what's more, she likes poetry – like me.

Maybe we have more in common than I thought.

Charlie

I have a meeting with my tutor, Mr Mitchell, before registration. I've got three exams today – Maths, Biology, and French – and I didn't really sleep last night. Waj reckons I'll make way more money with him than I ever could with a proper job, and I'm starting to wonder why I'm bothering.

All my teachers, like Mr Mitchell, keep telling me I could do really well, even apply to university. What they don't get is, even if I wanted to go, even if my dad got a job or, more likely, I robbed a bank, nobody from round 'ere ever amounts to owt, unless they become a Premier-ship footballer or win the lottery. I'm only OK at football and don't play the lottery – so basically, I'm fucked.

I get to school early and wait outside the staff room for Mr Mitchell. He's having a fag. They still smoke in the staff room, even though they're not allowed.

'Good morning, Charles,' he says, sticking his head round the door. The smell of instant coffee wafts into the corridor then up my nose, causing me to wretch. 'I won't be a second . . . '

Ten minutes later – they love to keep you waiting, teachers – Mr Mitchell leads me into the canteen, which is empty. All the chairs are on the tables and the kitchen shutters are closed. He pulls down two chairs for us to sit on.

'I'm gonna get a Coke,' I say, walking over to the vending machine.

'How are you feeling?' he asks when I sit down, tilting his head to the side, to show he cares.

Mr Mitchell's quite young, for a teacher, and I've heard some of the girls whispering about how fit he is. I don't see it myself. He wears suit jackets with jeans, probably 'cause he thinks it's cool. It's not.

'Reet,' I shrug, cracking open my can. It spurts and I wrap my lips round it, sucking at it until it stops. Mr Mitchell smiles at me and I smile back without thinking, then look away.

'Are you prepared?' he asks, a bit flustered after the silence.

There's some more while I think of the right thing to say.

'Suppose,' is all I can manage.

'Well, Charles – '

'It's Charlie,' I interrupt. 'Call me Charlie, sir.'

'Well,' he says, pulling his face in a proper weird way, 'I'd prefer to address you by your full name – '

'That *is* my full name,' I interrupt again. 'I mean, I was christened Charlie. Not Charles.'

I look away again, first at the table and my half-finished can of Coke, then out the window at the blossom trees, where the Sixth Formers sit at dinner.

'I see,' he says. 'I did not . . . know that . . . '

I finish my Coke and crumple the can in one hand, before spinning it round and round on the table in front of us.

'OK . . . *Charlie*,' he carries on, emphasising my name like there's now some sort of connection between us, even though he's just calling me by my proper name. 'I just wanted to wish you good luck and tell you that if you want to go over anything, before the English exam on Friday, then you can. Not that I think you'll need my help. I'm sure you're going to do very well . . . '

'No pressure then,' I mumble, not looking at him.

'Sorry?'

'Is that all?' I say, now looking straight at him.

'Yes, well . . . I, I suppose,' he stutters, before recovering. 'Yes, that's all.' I go to leave. 'Good luck, Charlie.' He stands up and holds out his hand for me to shake.

'Thanks, sir,' I say, shaking it before doing one as fast as I can.

Hayley

I've had two exams already and now I'm sitting in the assembly hall, tap-tapping my pen on the desk and waiting for another to start.

The other two didn't go well. I couldn't do most of the Maths questions so just left them, and Biology was proper hard, all questions on summat called 'rattus rattus' and plants and stuff like that.

Brooker and Digger are messing round at the front and they have to be separated. Then, about twenty minutes in, Brooker stands up and leaves. He's grinning, like he's really pleased with himself. He can't have answered the questions, I think, proper panicking.

The next hour flies by, but I'm over halfway through so start to calm down a bit. My trouble's the timing. I always start slow then have to rush at the end. Fifteen minutes before it's over, though, I'm finished. I can't believe it. I check over my answers. Yep, I'm done.

I walk out the assembly hall and past reception, so happy 'cause I've never finished an exam before the end. Someone shouts my name as I reach the main doors.

'Hayley!' the voice sounds again. I turn and see the voice belongs to Mr Mitchell, who's standing in front of the hall doors.

'Erm . . . sorry, sir . . . ' I walk back towards him, red-faced and trying not to make eye contact.

'No *I'm* sorry, Hayley . . . ' he starts, before trailing off. He seems nervous and doesn't look at me.

'What is it, sir?' I say, after a bit of silence. I'm not going to run away this time, I decide – for one thing I'm wearing knickers – so I look right at him.

'I just wanted to know if . . . whether you were planning on coming to the cramming session tomorrow, after school . . . in my room . . . '

The dirty perv! So, the bending over trick *did* work.

'I can do, sir,' I say, trying not to burst out laughing. 'If it's not too much trouble . . . '

'Not at all,' he says, making eye contact with me now, and even smiling. 'I think,' he says, lowering his voice, 'you would benefit, from a *session* . . . '

This day just keeps getting better and better, I think as I push through the main doors. I'm so happy I didn't reply to his text message now. Treat 'em mean, keep 'em keen.

I'm well pleased with myself but not looking where I'm going, 'cause I walk right into the back of a lad on the steps. He turns round. It's Charlie.

'Alreet,' is all he says. I can't speak, and end up just staring at him. 'You OK?' he asks. 'You look like you've seen a ghost.'

'Thanks,' I blurt out, before wishing I hadn't.

'Oh no, soz,' he says, smiling. 'I didn't mean it like that . . . '

I can't think of owt to say and there's a bit of an awkward silence.

'D'you wanna share this?' he says, finally. He passes me summat and I realise it's a joint. I've never done one before and it's all long and thick at the end, not like a ciggy.

'Erm, OK . . . ' I take it off him. It tastes funny but I don't feel any different.

'How was it for you?' he asks, smiling.

70

'I don't think it worked,' I say, confused.

He just looks at me, frowning. 'How about the exam then?'

'Oh OK, I think . . . erm . . . ' I trail off. I'm such an idiot.

'I thought it was hard but it didn't take that long. Y'never know do you?'

'No y'never know do you?' Great, now I'm just repeating what he says.

I stand there, desperately trying to think of summat else, but before I can Jenny Catlow bursts through the doors with a load of other people and rushes over to Charlie. She gives me the shit eye and I realise that's my cue, so I start to slip away, invisible again.

'Hayley!' calls a voice. I turn round and see it's Charlie. 'Another time, eh?' He smiles and gestures with the joint, and I smile back.

He noticed me – I mean, actually noticed me – and we had a connection.

CHAPTER TEN

Russell

What is love?

Or, what is it to love?

To love is to give up something of yourself for another – *for* the love of another.

What is the love of another?

The love of another is a promise – not of affection, which can change over time, but devotion. The love of another just is.

What is it to be?

To be is to exist in the moment, in the here and now, and to feel that existence like an overbearing and burdensome weight. That is to be.

To love is to give up something for the love of another.

The love of another is.

To be is not only to exist, but to understand and feel that existence.

So what is love?

Love is an overbearing and burdensome weight.

I spent most of my Biology exam writing because I finished early. It was multiple-choice and I had to just guess some of it, but I didn't want to leave in case people noticed me.

I was thinking of you, by the way.

The last time we slept together in the same bed – as friends, of course – was on your thirteenth birthday. A car had hit your dog. He'd tried to crawl back home but only made it as far as the front lawn. You'd found him there after getting home from school and made your mum take him to the vet's, but you both knew that he was dead.

That night, you'd called me in tears and asked if you could come over. We watched *Dirty Dancing*, your favourite, and fell asleep on my bed.

In the middle of the night, I woke up and you were sitting on my floor, your knees against your stomach, crying. I didn't even think. I just put my arms around you and held you until you stopped.

What happened next was, thinking back now, your way of saying thank you. For being there, I suppose. I'd never done anything with a girl – not even a kiss. You'd kissed plenty of boys at primary school and at high school went out with an older boy, Scott, who had a car but was on the dole and a complete and utter moron.

You got into bed with me and took off my undies. It was the first time I'd ever been naked in front of someone other than my mum, and I was really embarrassed. It was so hard that I thought I was going to explode, but you just stroked me gently. I went to sleep happy, thinking that you were now my girlfriend.

The next morning, though, you were in a sleeping bag on the floor.

Charlie

I'm in the park with Ish and a few lads from the gym. We've been kicking a ball about since we got out of school,

73

but they're all knackered now. Fucking useless. For lads that go the gym nearly every day, they're proper unfit. After a bit of running about, they're all wiped out lying on the grass, smoking.

I let them know I've got to be off and make my way to the bus station, seein' as it's gone 5. I had a late exam 'cause, unlike everyone else, I do German as well as French, and now I really need to get home 'cause I'm off out later with Waj. He said he'd pick me up but I didn't really want him turning up at my house, knowing what my dad's like, so I need to get home, change then make my back across town – and I can't afford to mess about.

I end up waiting in the station with Jenny 'cause she cornered me after my exam. She must've waited for me, again, and it's obvious she didn't get the message I don't want to hang round with her.

As luck'd have it, though, this woman comes over and starts asking her all these questions, stopping her from bothering me. She's BNP, a Union Jack pin on her blouse, a load of leaflets in her hand.

'D'yer catch this bus every day, love?' she says. She's small and chubby, half her teeth rotten. A chain-smoker, that's for sure.

'Every day,' says Jenny. 'Are they changin' it or summat? Is that why yer askin' questions? It's not regular enough as it is, so I 'ope they're gonna make it come on time.'

I see my bus and slip away as the woman starts talking again. 'I know . . . the whole area's in decline int it?' she says, like she's not even listening. 'I don't mind the Asians, but they wear full dress round 'ere. I 'ave a friend what

74

lives in Manchester and she says they don't wear full dress there. I think it's down to education . . . '

I get in to find my mum scrubbing the floor again.

'Mum,' I whisper, crouching down and kissing her on the forehead, 'is Dad home yet?'

'No I don't think so, Charlie,' she says, not looking at me. I think I could've asked her owt and she would've said that.

'You had any tea yet?' I say, chucking my bag on the kitchen table next to Mum's handbag. It's open and there's a leaflet sticking out. It says *Are you afraid of your partner?* on the front but I can't read the rest. She must've picked it up from the doctor's this morning, when she went about her back.

If my dad helped round the house she wouldn't have a fucking bad back. The doctor doesn't know that, course, so he keeps giving her all these painkillers that turn her into a zombie most of the time.

'No I don't think so, Charlie . . . '

'You not hungry Mum?'

'I'm fine,' she says, staring at summat on the floor. 'I'm fine . . . ' She trails off and starts humming the theme tune from *Antiques Roadshow*.

I go over to the freezer and take out two chicken Kievs, before turning the oven to gas mark seven. I check my phone again and see I've got just under an hour before I need to be back out again, so I run upstairs and lock myself in the bathroom. I feel proper horny in the shower but don't have time, so get out and dry myself, dress quickly and run back downstairs. The oven's not hot

75

enough yet, so I run back upstairs, put some gel in my hair, faff with it a bit then splash some aftershave on my neck. When I get back down, the oven's hot enough so I chuck in the Kievs, set the timer for twenty minutes and put the kettle on.

'Fancy a brew, Mum?'

She's still scrubbing the floor and doesn't hear me, so I make her one anyway. When the Kievs are done, I set them down on two plates and walk over to her.

'Mum, I've made you summat,' I say, crouching down again. She looks at me, confused. 'Come and sit wi' me.'

'Oh thanks, Charlie,' she says, struggling to get up. 'I'm starving . . . ' I put one hand on a bony shoulder and the other under a bony arm, helping her up.

We sit at the table for a while, just eating the Kievs and drinking our tea. Sometimes, when we're like this, I think what it'd be like if I'd never come along, if Mum and Dad'd be happier. Mum lost two kids at birth before me, and she always calls me her 'miracle baby'. Well, when I was little, before everything took a turn for the worse.

I look across the table and see she's got tears in her eyes. I reach out and put my hand on hers as one big tear drops on her plate. She only moves away when she hears the back door slam, and she doesn't need to say owt for me to know my dad's home.

'Well int this cosy?' he says, scoffing. 'I'm out lookin' for work all day and I come 'ome to this? I'm alright Jack, cast off the boat!'

Mum jumps up and goes back to the bucket and sponge, scrubbing the floor again, as I get my arse over to the freezer.

'Sorry Dad, erm, I didn't know when you were gettin' back. I'll make you summat now . . . '

'Look at this,' he carries on, standing at the sink and pointing at the washing up bowl. 'No pots've bin done.' He walks back towards the oven. 'And look!' he shouts, striding over Mum. 'The floor's filthy . . . '

'I'll do it now,' I say, leaving the freezer door open and walking past him, towards the sink.

'Don't interrupt me lad,' he says, shoving me so hard I end up back at the freezer. I stand there for a moment, frozen, until he looks away. 'What 'bout tea? *She's* not gonna meck it is she? Look at state of 'er!'

'The oven's on. I'll put a chicken pie in for you. I'm goin' out soon – '

'Who wi'?' he interrupts. He's standing next to me at the sink now, and I can smell the booze on him. 'Don't think I don't know what yer tryin' on lad. If I find out yer've bin 'angin' round wi' wrong sort, there'll be trouble.'

'I'm just goin' out wi' . . . Brooker and Digger . . . and that . . . ' I even look at him, so he thinks I'm telling the truth.

'Sound lads, them,' he says, his voice calmer now. Sound as a pound . . . ' He trails off and staggers into the front room.

I finish the washing up, which doesn't take long 'cause there's not much to do, then put the pie in the oven, setting the timer for thirty minutes.

'It'll be ready in half an hour, Dad,' I say, loud enough for him to hear in the front room.

When I turn round, though, he's standing right in front

of me. He leans in close so I can smell the whisky on his rank breath. 'Where d'yer get these from?' he says, holding a new pair of Rockports in his hand.

I've been putting some of the money Waj gives me towards bills and that, and trying to get rid of the rest without it looking obvious. Problem is, there's so fucking much of it and, to make things worse, Waj just buys me stuff anyway.

'I've been workin', Dad, after school . . . like you told me to.' I'm backing against the oven, sweating. 'I just wanted to help out, and I had a bit leftover. My others got nicked . . . by some Paki lads, at school . . . '

'Yer mark my words, lad,' he says, coming closer, a demonic grin on his face. 'If I find out yer lyin' to me, yer'll wish yer'd not. Yer remember what I told yer 'bout liars, don't yer?'

I nod, but then he grabs me by the throat.

'If I find out yer lyin',' he carries on, slurring his words, 'yer'll . . . wish . . . yer'd . . . never . . . bin . . . born.'

Hayley

Jenny Catlow jumps me in the bus station. She's waiting for the same bus and, as soon as I sit down, she stands over me, making sure I'm scared. I am, too, 'cause I've heard she's a bit mental.

'I saw yer talkin' to Charlie outside school yesterday,' she says. 'Don't think I've not noticed yer stalkin' him and followin' him 'bout and that.'

'I don't know w – '

'Shut the fuck up, bitch!' she interrupts, her voice loud

enough to startle people waiting. 'He's not interested in girls like *you*.'

'What d'you mean?' I say, squirming in my seat.

'*Virgins*!' She shouts it and I look round, feeling myself go red. 'He wouldn't go near a fridge like *you*. So stay away, or else.'

I don't want to catch the same bus as her so wait for the next one, and I end up missing Dad 'cause he's working lates. I don't bother making owt to eat 'cause I'm not hungry, so I just climb into bed and cry all the way through *Dirty Dancing*, singing along like a right saddo.

Now *that's* love, I think, turning out my lamp.

I picture Mr Mitchell as my eyes start to stick together. He was a bit touchy feely after school, but he didn't try owt on. I think he's quite sweet really, and it's not like he's a paedo. I *am* sixteen, remember, and he's probably only about thirty.

Next time, though, I'll make sure he *does* try it on. I'll show Jenny Catlow she's not the only one who can get a bloke. She thinks she's got Charlie wrapped round her little finger, but she's no better than me.

CHAPTER ELEVEN

Russell

People stare and start edging away, slowly. Then they laugh.

'What are you looking at?' I mutter under my breath, to nobody in particular.

I've had a bad day and, even though I keep telling myself that it was only one stupid exam, that there'll be others, I can't help myself.

In one swift movement I kung fu kick a McDonald's cup off the top of an overflowing rubbish bin, in front of where I stand. Pacing up and down at the scene of the crime, the act of littering glaringly obvious to that judgemental lot at the bus stop, I then shove the bin with my foot, at first tentatively, before knocking it over completely with a second, this time unstoppable, kick. Unsure of what to do next, I glance at the people at the bus stop, still staring at me. I pick up the bin, the base first, followed by the top, and some of the rubbish strewn across the pavement. Then I wipe my hands, which are covered in bin juice, on my school trousers, and immediately regret it. I look around again. People have now lost interest. The bus pulls up to the stop and, after waiting my turn, I get on, walking straight to the back. It's not the school bus, so I should be OK.

I really messed up my French today. I just couldn't remember the verbs. People always tell you that can happen but I never believed it, until now. I stare out of the window and try to forget about it, but all I can think of is how badly the other exams must have gone too. I thought that I'd done OK in History, even Chemistry, which I'm not that good at, but after the event I'm suddenly doubting it, convincing myself that I made mistakes, misinterpreted the questions somehow.

The bus passes some shops, and the whole row is boarded up except for the Army recruitment centre. That'll be me when I fail all of my exams, I think with a shudder.

We stop and a man comes to the back, sitting down opposite me. He didn't get on just now, though. I watched him move from the front of the bus when people got on. I look away, out of the window, hoping he's not moved to talk to me.

'Fuckin' hell . . . ' he says, quietly.

It's just as I thought. He's said this to strike up a conversation, trying to make a connection. His tone is hopeful, and not aggressive in any way.

I look at him without thinking, because I can't help it, but thankfully he's staring down at his feet. At first glance, he appears to have long yellow hair. Look closer, though, and his white roots are visible. He's wearing a suit jacket, shirt and trousers, but still looks dishevelled. Maybe it's because he's unshaven, I think, watching him. He looks up, his eyes darting around inside his head, looking for that connection.

This man is lonely, I think, looking away again and avoiding his gaze for the next few minutes. This man is sad. But I don't want to talk to him, because he's drunk. The desire to ignore him is overwhelming. I start to panic, willing the bus to reach the next stop so that I can get off and catch the one behind instead.

Then it occurs to me, as the doors slam shut and I look back, the man's eyes now connecting with mine. Is *he* a freak, an outcast? Or am I?

'Fuckin' hell . . . '

Charlie

I'm listening to 'Confused' by Simon Baker on the new iPhone Waj bought me, but it's too loud. I turn it down as a car passes the bus stop. A little girl's staring out the window. At first I think she's staring at me, then I realise she's daydreaming. Eyes wide, mouth open. Not a care in the world.

Three people are waiting for the same bus as me. Two of them – older lads, one in a red hat, the other shaven-headed – are playing with a mobile phone. They sound pissed. The other, standing a bit away from us, is wearing headphones. It's dark and starting to piss it down. I look at the one standing alone and we make eye contact, but he doesn't hold my stare. He looks lonely – he always does. I know him from school but I don't recognise the other two, and I realise he's not with them and doesn't know them either.

The bus arrives and I follow the two lads, then the lonely boy, upstairs. There's no one else on the top-deck. The lonely boy sits at the front, like he's driving, the way you used to when you were little. I sit down near the two lads, who are still playing with the mobile phone, and check mine.

After a bit, one of them clocks my iPhone. I just stare back, waiting for him to catch me.

'What *you* lookin' at?' he says, all cocky. I carry on staring at him, not saying owt.

He laughs and looks away, before looking back. I'm still staring.

'Oi mate, what the fuck are you lookin' at?' He's angry, trying to suss me out. 'You a fuckin' bender or summat?' I just laugh but his mate, fucking Roger Red Hat, still not looking up from the mobile phone, grabs his arm.

'Leave it,' he says. 'Look at this . . . ' The lonely boy looks over his shoulder at me, then at the lads. 'I think that boy's lookin' at you, though.'

Angry does stand up this time. 'What *you* lookin' at?' he screams at the lonely boy.

'Erm, nothing . . . ' he says, his voice quivering.

He looks at me again, then turns to face the other way, no doubt hoping that'll be the end of it. He eyes up the stairs to his right, like he's thinking about doing one.

'Yeah I think he's lookin' at you and all,' I say, staring at Angry. 'What you gonna do about it? You gonna sort him out?' I start laughing and the lonely boy looks at me again, panicked.

'Look mate,' Angry says, 'what the fu – '

'Look *mate*,' I interrupt, 'you see me lookin' then that boy lookin', and you wanna play the big man, but you do nowt about it. Well, I'm still lookin' at you, and so is he. What you gonna do about it?'

'He's pissed,' says Red Hat, not looking up from the phone. 'Leave it. It's not worth it . . . '

'You wanna know what I think?' I say to Angry, turning in my seat so I'm facing him.

'What?' he shouts back, still standing and refusing to take his mate's advice.

'I think you're scared of that boy. I think you talk a good game but, deep down, you're a soft cunt.'

'I don't know what he's going on about,' says the lonely boy, scared and suddenly sensing he should open his gob. 'I'm just – '

'Course you do,' I interrupt, looking at him and smiling. 'That's why you were lookin' at him, at the bus stop. I saw you. You agree with me. You think he's a soft cunt and all.'

'D'you wanna start summat?' says Angry, not sure who to confront.

'Chill the fuck out, pal. I'm just tellin' you what I saw. He was starin' at you, at the bus stop. He thinks you're a dickhead.'

'Is that right mate?' He's now staring at the lonely boy, who looks like he's about to start crying his eyes out.

He moves towards the front of the bus and the lonely boy, realising what's happening, jumps up, pulls his bag from under the seat and makes a run for the stairs, but he gets caught on a rail and the lad catches up to him.

Before he can swing, though, I grab him from behind and smack him in the side of the face. As I move towards him he scrambles to his feet and down the stairs. Fucking chicken shit.

'Thank you,' the lonely boy says, after a bit. 'Erm, my name's – '

'Russell,' I stop him, walking back to my seat. 'I know who you are.'

I stare at Red Hat as I put my headphones back in. He's just sitting there, though, not bothered, and still looking at that fucking phone.

Hayley

I creep downstairs just after midnight 'cause I can't sleep. Dad's not in bed, though. He's on the settee in his work clothes, and there's a half-eaten takeaway on the floor by his feet. He must've just got in and flopped down right there.

I go over to him and give him a kiss, accidentally waking him.

'Oh I'm sorry Daddy,' I whisper.

'That's OK sweet 'eart,' he whispers back, his eyes only half-open. 'I'm just glad yer 'ome. My little girl . . . '

I go upstairs and get back in bed, turning on the telly. It's late and there's nowt on so I turn on the computer. I have a look at ASOS, not that I can buy any of the nice things on there, then sign into Facebook.

Gemma tagged a photo from when we did a play at primary school. We were in the Nativity, and I played Mary – the star, if you don't count Jesus. I untag it 'cause I look so stupid, then start to look at people I might know.

There was a thing on the news about a girl copying someone else's profile and pretending to be them. I think, wouldn't that be cool, if you could just take someone else's glamorous life and be them for a while.

Sometimes I just search for names I see in fashion

magazines, the kind you think must have proper amazing lives. I type in 'Suki', a name I found when I was waiting at the dentist's the other day. There's one girl with an open profile, and she's got about two thousand photos of herself. She's seventeen, really skinny and pretty, and says she's a model with a part-time job at Topshop. I've always wanted to go Topshop in Manchester, 'cause the one in town's proper rubbish, but Gemma won't pay the bus fare and I've got no one else to go with.

I get bored of looking, a bit jealous to be honest, so climb into bed and soon start to feel sleepy. I've only got my English Lit exam left and there's not much point revising. Not after what happened with Mr Mitchell today.

I found a poem earlier, in my bag. He must've slipped it in there when I went to his cramming session. I've never been given owt like that before and it was so beautiful, about love and his feelings.

Oh no Hayley, I think as I drift off, a big smile on my face. I don't think you have owt to worry about there.

Love is an overbearing and burdensome weight.

CHAPTER TWELVE

Russell

Charlie saved my life tonight. I don't have anyone to tell so I thought I'd just tell you.

It was like one of those adventures I used to have. Do you remember? I'd dream up wild things when I was in bed, like the time I imagined I was with a girl and we were on the run from ninjas. We had to hide in a forest under a canopy, the rain coming down hard and the ninjas in pursuit.

That was when I used to kiss my pillow, for practice. I'm so stupid. I should've just asked you.

One night, I was kissing my pillow and I started touching myself. Suddenly, and without warning, I felt a rush deep inside and sat up, the feeling building until I fired it all the way across the room. I'd never had an orgasm before, and I woke up the next day to find the dried evidence all over my Gordon the Gopher.

I thought about that the other day actually. Mum's started putting my old cuddly toys back on my bed, even though I don't sleep with them anymore. I used to have to kiss each one an equal amount of times goodnight, before placing them neatly on the floor by my bed.

Anyway, I was telling you about Charlie. I was on the bus and this lad, this really frightening lad, was going to beat me up, but Charlie stood up for me. You should've seen how hard he hit him.

It made me think of that time when I had to be rescued from the toilets at school, when I was little. I suppose I've always been the type that needs rescuing, eh?

Why am I telling you this? I bet it didn't mean anything. So what if he knew my name? *And?* We *have* been at the same school for the last five years.

It's not as if you can hear me either. Look, I'm sorry that I wrote the poem for Hayley but, like I said, I was writing it for you really. It's not as if you can read the rubbish I write anyway. It's not as if you're going to write back.

I didn't cry, you know, after your accident. I still call it an accident because that's what your mum and dad called it, even after the post-mortem. They must've known. Nobody drowns in a bath by accident.

I knew that you were taking stuff, though. Your house was full of prescription pills because of your mum's depression, so it wasn't hard for you to get hold of a bit of diazepam without anyone noticing. I hear that all the kids are doing it now, but I bet they don't wash it down with Nitol like you did.

I didn't cry, but only because I knew that you were happy. That you just wanted to escape. I hope you know this, and don't think that it was because I didn't care. If you were here, now, I'd tell you that I cared.

Charlie

Waj has taken me with him to collect off this junky who owes him big time. I didn't really fancy it much to be honest, what with the stories Ish comes out with, but I couldn't exactly say that could I.

We pull up to a council estate in the centre of town, near the old mills. It's funny. In some places, factories have been turned into fancy flats. Not round 'ere. They're just left to crumble and fall down.

Waj hasn't said a word to me since we set off, but he seems to know where he's going so I just follow. He leads the way up about a million steps to the fifth floor, and I'm knackered by the time we get to a dingy-looking flat at the far end of a long, drafty walkway. Fuck knows why we couldn't just use the lift.

He bangs on the door and we wait. It's past ten but there's still plenty of noise coming from most of the flats – the ones that are occupied anyway. A lot are boarded up, some with sheets of metal.

He bangs again, this time louder.

'I 'eard yer first time,' says a voice. A woman opens the door, on the chain, and sticks her head round.

'We've come to see Gaz,' says Waj. 'Where is he?'

'He's not in . . . ' she answers, then tries to shut the door but Waj sticks his foot in the way and, with his other leg, kicks it open.

It must've knocked her back 'cause she's on her arse when we walk in. She's wearing a dressing gown but it's open so I can see her bony chest and the sores on her body. Her arms are all ruptured veins and dried blood.

'Look *bitch*,' says Waj, firm and frightening, even to me, 'tell me where he is or I'll break your arm.' He's gripping the woman's wrist behind her back and holding her down on the floor. Her dressing gown's hanging off completely now and I can see she's naked under it. 'Or do you want me to fuck your arse to get you to talk, loosen that tongue of yours?' Waj has his hand between her legs and she's trying to scream, but he's forced her face down on the carpet.

I want to say summat but he glares at me, so I keep it shut. I look round and see the flat's filthy, empty cans of lager and pizza boxes and shit everywhere.

'OK OK,' she says, after Waj lifts her so she can speak. 'He's in t' Weavers.' Waj gets to his feet and we start to make our way out. 'Please don't tell him I said owt,' she carries on, blocking our exit. She's crying. 'I'm dead if yer do . . . '

'You're dead anyway sweet heart,' says Waj, his voice calm, before shoving her out the way and slamming the door.

The Weavers is a rough pub round the corner from the flats. When we turn up it's pretty empty, like most pubs round 'ere.

'You can wait outside,' says Waj as we both spot this junky type – skinny, scruffy, skin hanging off – standing at the bar. 'You don't need to see this.'

I do as he says but, after just twiddling my thumbs for a bit, decide I'd rather see what's what than miss out on the action, so I make my way back in. I can't see Waj straight away, and this bloke with a skinhead and chunky gold chain is talking to an old woman at the bar, where the junky was before. She's wearing a proper slaggish dress and has a massive peroxide quiff.

'Last time I saw that hairstyle it were on *Dallas*!' the bloke says, laughing and turning his back on the old woman, leaving her alone at the bar.

She looks crushed, even though I bet she must be getting

used to it by now. We make eye contact as I pass and I'm about to smile at her, but she looks away and down at her feet instead.

I make my way round the other side. The junky's now sitting at the bar. He's talking to Waj but I'm not close enough to hear, so I try and get closer without Waj noticing. The junky's drumming his fingers in front of him. Waj is talking but he just laughs then points his finger, prodding Waj in the chest, before going back to drumming on the bar.

Then Waj looks at me, like he did back in the flat, and I freeze. He isn't angry, though, and actually smiles.

A second later, in a flash, Waj takes out a blade and stabs the junky's hand to the bar, twisting his other arm behind his back and causing him to make a sound I've never heard a human make before. A few people look round but not one says a word. Apart from the junky, course.

I think, watching this happen, you've got to be a particular type of person to go in for all this. You've got to want to destroy things.

Waj doesn't say owt in the car until we get back to mine. There aren't any lights on and I'm a bit relieved but, as I'm getting out the car, Waj grabs my arm.

'Next time I tell you to wait outside,' he says, looking at me with a coldness I've not seen before tonight, 'make sure you do it.'

'OK,' I say, nodding and making sure to look him in the eye.

He drives away and I shudder, realising the light in our front room's come on.

Hayley

I wake up in the middle of the night. I was having a dream – not about Mr Mitchell, but about Charlie.

He's following me but I'm acting like I don't know he's there. I'm on my way somewhere, I dunno, somewhere in the country I think.

Then suddenly we're in the middle of nowhere, surrounded by all these fields, standing face to face.

'I saw you in a dream,' he says, his voice different, y'know, a bit weird. It's Charlie, but he doesn't sound himself.

'What was I doing?' I ask.

'You were smiling sweetly.'

'Where was I?'

'You were standing in a field, like this. It was a sunny day.'

'What did I look like?'

'A breeze was blowing and your hair, golden and wild, was moving gently.'

'Why was I there?'

'You were walking towards me. I was walking backwards, filming you. I was telling you the camera loved you and this was making you laugh. I was telling you I loved you. You were telling me you loved me, too. I was telling you not to say "too". You were smiling sweetly. You looked so young . . . '

'Then what happened?'

'You turned and ran away. I ran after you, still filming. You ran through the field to a river and took off your dress. You looked back at me. You were smiling sweetly . . . '

He smiles and leans forward, like he's about to kiss me.

But before it can happen everything changes and we're standing on a terraced street. It's not my street but I recognise it from somewhere, maybe from near my house.

When I look at him, his face has changed. He's not smiling no more but scowling, his face battered and bloody.

'You were smiling sweetly. You looked so young, so pure . . .'

That's all I remember, though, 'cause that's when I wake up, proper drenched in a cold sweat.

CHAPTER THIRTEEN

Russell

It's everyone's last exam today and I've finished with only five minutes to go. I don't want to get up now, though, in case people notice me.

The usual suspects, Brooker and Digger, started talking halfway through before Mr Blackburn, the Art teacher who wears a plastic Batman tie, because he's an Art teacher I suppose, threw them out. They didn't care. They got a few laughs and that's what counts. To them, anyway.

A funny thing happened at the beginning of the exam, before Brooker and Digger started messing around. Mr Mitchell was making sure everyone had their pens and stuff in clear plastic bags. They make you do that so you don't bring notes in, but I still see people with things written on their hands. I don't know why. It's not as if you can write an essay about Jane Austen on the back of your hand.

So, this funny thing that happened. Mr Mitchell was checking everyone's plastic bags, but when he got to Hayley's desk he paused, as if she'd asked him a question, then as he walked away he placed his hand, just for a second, on hers.

Mr Mitchell's young, for a teacher, and I've heard that some of the popular girls fancy him. There's also a rumour that he got involved with a Third Year. I'm not sure, though. He's into that whole suit jacket with jeans look, and I doubt a girl like Hayley would be interested in someone like him.

No way, I think as I watch him slither past again. She's not that kind of girl.

'OK everyone, time's up,' he says, rocking back and forth on his tip-toes. I watch him closely, in case he makes eye contact with her or gives her some kind of signal, but then she stands up and walks out of the Hall.

I'm still staring at her, as she grabs her bag and pushes through the main doors, when Mr Mitchell appears by the side of my desk.

'Everything OK, Russell?'

'Erm . . . yes I think so, sir. Well, at least I finished anyway . . . ' I stand up, and start to follow everyone out.

'Good luck with your results,' he says. I turn back, and he nods. 'I'm sure that, if you keep your head down, things will work out just fine for you. If you keep your head down.' He doesn't take his eyes off mine, but narrows them, just slightly, then smiles.

'Yes, sir,' I say, turning to leave and already playing the exchange back in my head, again and again.

'Just keep your head down, Russell,' I whisper, when I get to the exit. 'Keep your head . . . '

Charlie

It was my last exam today and I'm in a rush 'cause I'm off out again tonight.

Waj is driving a few of us over to Manchester. He doesn't drink so we can all go out there, get lashed then drive back to his. It's a decent night in Manchester. The bars are better and there's no atmosphere. Go out round 'ere on a Friday night and you're likely to get into a scrap, just by looking at someone the wrong way. Call me a spoil sport but sometimes you just want to go out and have a laugh, without bashing someone.

I end up sitting next to Jenny on the bus home.

'What happened to your eye?' she says, reaching out to touch my face.

'Nowt,' I say, flinching then looking out the window.

I got it in the neck from my dad the other night, when Waj dropped me off. It didn't take him long to realise where I've been getting all my money from, and he gave me a pasting – the kind I've not had in a long time. He only stopped when I told him I'll give him a cut, on top of what I'm already putting towards bills.

My mum got it worse, though. She tried to stick up for me, then he used his rings on her. I called the police but, when I went back in their bedroom, Mum was cowering in the corner and he'd done one. The fucking pigs said they couldn't come straightaway, but he wasn't taking any chances.

'*You* been avoidin' me?' I look at her and she smiles. 'I've bin thinkin' 'bout yer . . . '

I don't answer and she thumps me on the arm.

'What yer doin' tonight? Wanna come out in town, y'know, to celebrate exams finishin' and that?'

'Nah,' I say, looking out the window again. 'I'm goin' Manchester actually – '

'Who wi'?' she interrupts, her voice loud.

'Oh just some mates. Some lads. You don't know 'em . . . '

'Ah, a lads' night out . . . that's OK then.'

I turn round and smile, before looking back out the window. There's a board outside a newsagent's with to-night's *Evening News* headline:

TOO POOR TO AFFORD TOMBSTONE
FOR DEAD TODDLER

'Y'know, I was beginning to think yer'd met someone and were, like, seein' another girl,' she carries on, laughing but not sounding too sure of herself.

'If only you knew, eh?' I say, blocking her out. 'If only you knew . . . '

Waj picks me up in front of the bus station. Ish gets out and sits in the back with Asif, so I can sit next to Waj. They've all got the face on for some reason. The exams are over and I'm chuffed, but we end up driving all the way into Manchester in silence – except for the CD player, which, as per, is too loud.

When we pass what used to be Boddington's, before they turned it into a car park, the CD stops and radio comes on in the middle of a story about teenage suicides. It was on the news last night, these kids from this one area of Wales all dropping like flies, and the police can't seem to understand why.

I went on this website where you can watch people doing it in front of webcams the other day. The weird thing is, they always try to keep their eyes open.

I try to listen in as the newsreader says summat about how websites like Facebook are to blame then someone else, I think a politician, says 'We've got to protect our children from the internet' but I can't listen to the rest 'cause Waj puts a new CD in.

We park in the NCP behind Kendal's. On our way out there's this homeless man sleeping on the steps.

'Wakey wakey!' Ish shouts, pulling on his sleeping bag.

'Have some fucking self-respect, Ish,' says Waj.

We carry on and walk along Deansgate, to the bar in the Hilton.

'This building looks like the new Samsung, innit?' says Asif as we make our way up in the lift. 'Don't you reck, Charlie lad?'

'No,' I say, not looking at him. 'No I fuckin' don't.'

The bar's pretty full but Waj seems to know everyone, and we're taken to a quiet area in the back. He orders JD and Cokes and just a Coke for himself, then lights a cigarette. Some people at nearby tables look at me but I just stare back, my expression blank, until they look away. Once I've necked a few, I start to feel like a menace.

After a bit, Waj starts explaining his new business plan. Not to Ish and Asif. They can't stop talking about those dead bodies that keep turning up.

'They better not mess with us, fuckin' gora,' Asif is saying. He's getting wound up, and cocky. 'This lad was gettin' fly down Powerhouse, and I told 'im innit. Don't fuck wit' us. Or y'know what happens – '

Waj grabs him by the shoulder and pulls him in close, so close I can't hear. When he lets go, Asif shuts the fuck up.

He turns back to me. We've been here for an hour now

and I'm too drunk to take it in properly, but it sounds like Waj is planning on pimping out his girls and dressing it up as a dating agency. He's given it a weird name – an Urdu word – and keeps stressing how he'd be offering men a service, showing them not just how to pick up any girl, but 'the most attractive girl in the room'.

'The girls on offer would be top quality,' he explains, 'and after coming to the workshops men would be able to pick them up with consummate ease.'

At some point, after another few, Waj admits that for 'a little extra' members would be able to pay to be with the girls anyway. I laugh when he says this, and he lights another cigarette.

'I'm telling you this because I see a lot of potential in you, Charlie,' he says, looking at me. 'My business is *my* business. I only share information with people I trust. Do you understand what I mean by trust, Charlie?'

'Yeah, Waj, I think so but – '

'I trust you because I know you're loyal,' he interrupts. He's smiling but not in a friendly way. 'I value loyalty above everything else, and anyone who's disloyal, well . . . ' He trails off at this point, then does an action like he's shooting me in the head with an imaginary shotgun. I get the message. 'Anyway,' he says, a lot calmer all of a sudden, 'we're meant to be having a night out, so let me cut to the chase.' He smiles again and grips my shoulder.

'What d'you mean?' I ask, not sure how to take him.

'I want you to try it out,' he says, looking round the room.

'Erm . . . what d'you mean?' I ask again, confused.

'Why do you think we're in this hotel?' he says, edging closer and looking right at me. 'I've got a girl waiting for you. You do like girls?' He laughs.

'But, erm . . . I have no cash on me . . . ' I say, lying.

'Don't worry about that, Charlie.' He stands, stubbing out his cigarette. 'This is on the house.'

I'm pissed by now but Waj helps me stagger out the bar, past these trendy people, all glossy and new up here in this hotel, on top of the world.

He bundles me into the lift and starts laughing but I don't know why, then we're in a different part of the hotel with no one about but us.

There's a long corridor and a proper blinding light hanging down from the ceiling, in a room with a bright red door. A girl, a lot younger than me, sits on a double bed, her legs crossed. She's thin with pale skin, big eyes and long blonde hair – so long it's almost down to the bed. She's holding a joint and looks up, offering it to me. I sit down on the bed next to her and take a drag. As I lie back, she stands up and takes off her dress, and I can't be sure but I don't think the door's closed and there might be someone else in the room, but my head's all over the place and I can barely focus. The girl walks over, slow, and straddles me, taking off my jeans and underwear. She lies back a bit and starts fingering herself. Her twat's hairless and looks soft and wet. Then she gets on top of me and I look up at her. She's closed her eyes and keeps them closed, but mine are open, always open, and I don't close them until I realise I'm not going to cum.

I turn my head to the side, not turned on, and hear

100

someone say something in the corner of the room, then the door slam, as I feel myself passing out.

Hayley

'All the jobs are goin' t' China,' Dad's saying. 'I've been on short time for months now . . . '

I'm spending another Friday night in, like a right loser, 'cause I've got no money. Dad's been giving me what he can, but it's barely enough for my bus fare let alone a night out.

'Mr Mitchell told me companies always try to make people work for less and less,' I say. 'What was he saying? Summat about wages . . . ' I trail off. I didn't really get it but then again I don't see him to learn, do I?

I won't be doing from now on anyway. It was my last exam today, so I suppose we'll have to find other ways to be together.

'That's nice sweet 'eart,' he says – *so* not listening.

'And you remember those slides what were on telly, in that art gallery in London?' I say, remembering another thing Mr Mitchell said and trying to sound confident. 'Well he also said the slides are art 'cause they're in a gallery . . . ' I trail off again, realising he's still not listening. The news has changed to summat about terrorists in Bradford, and he can't take his eyes off the screen.

'If they don't like it 'ere,' he says, suddenly proper angry, 'send 'em back where they cem from!'

'Does anyone want a brew?' Gemma asks, oblivious. She's sleeping here tonight and hovering over me, blocking my view of the telly 'cause she's so round.

'Y'know, I make tea but I don't drink it? I just don't like it that much really . . . ' She pauses, as if thinking about summat – 'contemplative', that's the word what Mr Mitchell uses to describe me – and every time she makes that face she gets a double chin. 'Every now and then, though,' she goes on, 'I'll have a cup of tea . . . '

'I'll 'ave a brew but get on wi' it Gems!'

She looks miffed and saunters off. I don't really care, though. I've had a good day and am not about to let that mard arse spoil it.

Mr Mitchell said he'd like to see me, outside school. He asked for my mobile number and I thought it was a bit weird that, 'cause of his text, but then again maybe he was just pretending to need it when he'd actually already got it from school.

Anyway, we've got all summer where he's not my teacher, and there'll be nothing to get in the way. He said he might take me away, too. I've never been anywhere to be honest, so that'd be amazing. Just us.

He's not like boys my age. He's so brainy and experienced, and the other night he picked me up and took me out to a restaurant, and he ordered me some wine and it was just really romantic. I've never done owt like it before.

It was an Italian restaurant in Colne, proper authentic with flags and music. Even the menus were foreign.

'So Hayley,' he said, topping up my glass. I'd already downed the first one, I was so nervous. 'What do you want to be when you grow up?' He smiled at me, but I knew he was joking.

'Cheeky!' I said, smiling then gulping down my wine.

'You know what I mean.'

He reached across the table, but pulled back when the waitress walked past. She was young, maybe just a bit older than me, and proper skinny but pretty with it. Typical blonde. She had these big boobs, too, making me feel like a right minger next to her. She'd been eyeing us up all night, and I don't think Mr Mitchell liked it.

'What do you want to do . . . next year?'

'I wanna go Drama school 'cause one day . . . ' I trailed off, feeling silly.

'Go on . . . ' he said, looking at the waitress. She was still staring, and it was putting me off.

'One day . . . no you're gonna think it's stupid.' I looked at the waitress, and thought for a minute she was smirking.

'Hayley just tell me,' he said, reaching across again and taking my hand in his. The waitress saw, and I started to think she looked jealous.

'I want to star in a musical, but a film – '

'Ah . . . ' he said, smiling. 'Like *Moulin Rouge*?'

'I knew you'd think it was stupid.'

'No I don't,' he said, interrupting again. 'I don't think it's stupid at all.' He looked at me then glanced over at the waitress, who was pouring wine at the next table – but obviously still listening in. 'If there's one thing I've learned in my life,' he carried on, 'it's that if you want something – I mean, really *want* something – you should just go for it.'

We went for a drive after, and kissed in a lay-by. He was

sweet, though, and didn't try owt on. We've done stuff together, but we've not gone that far yet.

Gemma brings my brew, and I start daydreaming about when I nearly lost my virginity to our paper boy. It was probably my first chance to do it with someone, but I reckon even if we'd really wanted to, and had got far enough to have a go, we were too young to know where to put everything anyway.

His name was Iain, a Third Year at school. He was our paper boy when we all lived up Harle Syke, and I had my room downstairs, and he used to knock on my window every Saturday morning in the summer holidays. We wouldn't talk much. We'd just snog, me leaning out my window, our mouths open and going round and round like two washing machines. It was nice that, just kissing. I liked him. He tasted of Irn-Bru bars.

We kept this up for weeks until, one day, he didn't knock, and I never saw him again. There was this horrible rumour he'd been raped by some boys on the football fields at school. Apparently they'd used a snooker cue.

I don't know if it was true – Mum died that August so I was all over the place – but he didn't come back to school at the end of summer.

PART TWO

CHAPTER FOURTEEN

Russell

Once upon a time, in a place where being different was to risk everything, there lived a boy. The boy's name was Russell Crackle, and he was in love.

Not with anyone in particular, you understand. No, Russell was in love with the idea of being in love. If you'd called him a 'Romantic', he'd have laughed in your face. But you wouldn't have been far off.

Russell didn't belong in this place. It wasn't big enough for him and, if he stayed, he wouldn't survive. But one day, with a bit of luck – because everyone needs luck don't they – Russell would escape . . .

'Russell!' my mum screams from downstairs.

I'm lying on my bed, daydreaming and listening to 'Working Class Hero' by John Lennon. I pull the headphones out of the socket so I can hear her but still listen to the song.

And you think you're so clever, and classless,

and free . . .

'Russell!' she screams again, ruining my favourite part of the song.

But you're still fucking peasants, as far as

I can see.

'What?' I scream back, opening my bedroom door about an inch and refusing to leave my room.

'Phone for yer.'

'Who is it?' I say, jumping up from my bed and leaning over the banister.

'Just come and get it will yer? I'm missing my *Eastenders . . .* '

I run downstairs and pick up the handset. The earpiece is covered in concealer – not from me, but only because I never get a phone call.

'Hello?' I say.

'Oh hullo sir, this is Mr Gash, first name Seymour, and I'm calling from the . . . '

I interrupt Jason by laughing, which causes him to laugh too.

'Nice try Jason!' My mum rolls her eyes and turns up the telly, so I take the handset up to my room.

'How you doing little man?' he says. 'I've just been speaking to your mum. She sounds well . . . '

'Erm, yeah . . . we're OK,' I say, not sure if he's being serious.

'Listen, I called because I wanted to run something by you. I've not mentioned it to your mum, so you'll have to do that, but it's something for you to think about. Promise me you won't say anything until you've talked to your mum and had a good think about it?'

'OK . . . '

'You promise to talk to your mum first?'

'Yes, Jason. I promise . . . '

'Promise?'

'Promise!' I say, excited. 'Just tell me.'

'That's three times you promised,' he says, laughing. Jason likes to re-enact scenes from *Fight Club*, his favourite film. He practically knows the script off by heart. 'OK well, you remember how I said you could stay with me, if you came to study here in Leeds?'

'Yeah . . . '

'I've been giving it a lot of thought and think you should come and stay for a few weeks, y'know, get out of that place for a while . . . '

'Jason that'd be – '

'Hang on,' he says, interrupting. 'That's not all. You remember I went to that college here in Leeds? Y'know, before my degree? Well, I've been in touch with them and they'd like to meet you, with a view to you going there next year to do A-Levels. They also do all sorts of creative courses – foundation courses they call them – and you can do that then do a degree after, if you want . . . '

'Russell!' My mum's on the phone, and shouts my name so loud I have to take the phone away from my ear.

'Mum what are y – '

'Russell, I need the phone. Yer can talk to Jason another time.'

'Hi Denise. Sorry to call at a bad – '

'Another time, Jason,' she interrupts. 'I need the phone.' She hangs up.

Charlie

I opened a bank account on my sixteenth birthday, just for the sake of it. My dad doesn't even have a bank account. He gets his benefits on a Giro and does cash in hand jobs – when he works, that is. Standing in front of the cash point, I start to smile. I bet most people round 'ere have fuck all in their bank accounts, course, but with the cash I'm making I really should have more than £16.61 in mine.

'You've not been paying your money into the bank have you?' Waj asks as we pull away fast, tires spinning. A song starts and it's typical Waj – old American funk and hip-hop, all that 70s shite – but he thinks he's educating me and, to be fair, he is the boss.

> *This country wants nostalgia.*
> *They want to go back as far as they can,*
> *Even if it's only as far as last week.*
> *Not to face now or tomorrow – but to face*
> > *backwards . . .*

'Course not,' I say, after a bit.

I've been putting the cash, and there's a lot, in an old Jaguar sports bag under my bed. No one ever goes in my room so it should be safe there, for now.

Waj just nods. I look out the window as we drive past the old shoe factory where Mum used to work, when she was about my age. It shut ages ago, course.

> *Nostalgia, that's what we want.*
> *The good ol' days – when we gave 'em hell . . .*

'I hate this place . . . ' he says – to himself, I think.

We're in the most run down part of town, and that's really saying summat round 'ere. The road we're on runs through what used to be a community, with a school, a doctor's surgery – all the things you'd expect. I can remember it when I was little 'cause it's not that far from us. My dad used to take me to the park on Sundays, to kick a ball about and that.

This ain't really your life,
Ain't really your life,
Ain't really, ain't nothing but a movie . . .

It's also where Roger lives. Roger's this older bloke I met about three years ago, when I first left home. He's the soundest person I know. Fuck knows why he lives round 'ere. Nearly all the houses left are boarded up or crumbling, the only factory's closed and there are no pubs anymore – just an off licence, that's it. There are these massive speed bumps everywhere and all, so you can take in the misery as you crawl along at ten mile an hour.

We pull up in front of a bit of land I think used to be a park but isn't owt anymore, just concrete and overgrown weeds. There's a row of maybe six terraced houses opposite, nowt either side, which looks a bit odd. Waj stops the car and turns to face me.

'I need you to collect,' he says, his voice calm. 'Go to number twelve and ask for Sandra. They'll tell you she's not in but they'll be lying, OK? It's a squat and she's a junky with too much junk. She'll definitely be in.'

I get out and find number twelve. There are a few lads, a bit older than me, messing round on bikes in front of the offy. They eye me up but I just stare back and nod. Then I bang on the door, nice and hard. Eventually, a woman answers through the letterbox.

Waj doesn't like dealing with this sort. They're what he calls 'the bottom of the pyramid'. He prefers the sort with money that live out of town – the ones that use pills and coke for a good time on a Saturday night, but drive an Audi TT in the week. Kids and junkies, he leaves to me.

'Is Sandra about?' I say, through the letterbox.

'You don't need to shout!' she shouts. 'And no, she's not. She's . . . well she's out, OK? Come back tomorro' . . . '

I step back and eye up the house. The windows are closed with metal shutters and I start to think about how they got in.

'Open the door,' I say, calm.

'She's not in,' she says. 'Fuckin' come back t – '

'Open the door,' I interrupt, my voice louder now, 'or when I go round the back and climb through the window, I'll cut your fuckin' nose off, cunt.'

I'm not bluffing. Not about the knife anyway. I've no idea if I'll get in through the back window – just a wild guess.

I step back and take the knife out my pocket, so she can see it through the letterbox. There are some voices, then the door opens.

'Don't shoot the messenger, OK?' the woman says. She's got badly bleached hair, black roots three inches deep, wearing a pink dressing gown with fluffy cuffs. 'She told me not to let anyone – '

'Yeah yeah. Where is she?'

'Upstairs,' she says, laughing, 'but she's shootin' up so I dunno how, y'know . . . '

I go upstairs, making sure to avoid two needles on the top step. The bathroom's right in front of me, the door open. Someone's sprayed diarrhoea all over the shop, and no fucker's bothered to clean it up.

I can hear noises in a room to my right, so walk in. It stinks and there's no furniture – just a candle and two people, one lad and a much younger girl who looks off her face, shagging on the floor.

'Oi fuck off will yer . . . ' the lad moans. He's a skinny, pale fucker, and looks gone and all.

'Where's Sandra?' I say, not moving.

'I said fuck – '

I stop him short by digging him in the back of the skull, then pull him off the girl, who just flops on the floor. She's skinny with cropped blonde hair, and passed out. I keep hold of the lad and start choking him from behind, so he can't move.

'Where's Sandra?' I say, my voice still calm.

'OK OK I'll tell yer!' His track marks look fresh, and I start to feel sorry for him. I look down at his cock and it's only half-hard and tiny. 'She's next door . . . '

I dump him on the floor and go in the next room. As promised, there's a girl in the room. There are a few candles strewn about but again no furniture. She's on her back and I spot a needle on the floor next to her.

'Waj sent me to collect, Sandra,' I say, standing over her. 'Where's the money, love?'

She doesn't say a word, just looks up at me, her eyes glazed over, then smiles. She looks like she probably used to be pretty but is so thin and sickly now – dark brown bags under bloodshot eyes, teeth brown and rotten – I can't bring myself to keep looking at her.

In the corner of the room's a pile of old magazines and videos. I walk over and pick up a couple of cases, realising they're empty. I try a few more – still empty – until I get to a copy of *Made in Britain*. It feels heavier than the others so I open it. Inside, there's only about two hundred in twenties. I always hated that film.

'Sandra,' I say, smiling at her 'cause she's still smiling at me, and despite the fact I know full well she's not on this fucking planet, 'Waj tells me you owe him three hundred, but I'm gonna give you a break.' I walk over to her and crouch down. 'I'll sort the rest out wi' him, OK?' She's still smiling at me as I stand up and walk towards the door. 'You're welcome . . . '

I get back in the car and hand Waj his £300, topped up with my own cash.

'Was there a girl in there?' he asks, driving off. 'I mean, a *young* girl . . . ?'

'She was just a little kid, Waj.'

'It's business,' he says, putting his foot down and cutting up a van at the roundabout. 'That junky in there, do you know who his dad is?'

'No, who?' I say, looking out the window.

'The local MP!' He starts laughing and reaches to change the CD.

'I've got summat actually,' I say, stopping him. 'Have a listen to this . . . '

I put in a CD this caner gave me the other day. Waj had sent me round to collect from him. He owed £250 but gave me £200 and the CD, telling me that this one track – 'The Don' – was worth every penny. I told him I was doing him a favour and not to get fly with me but, listening to it now, I reckon he had a point.

'Just park it and I'll go in,' I say as we pull into the car park and see the massive queue for the drive-thru bit. 'It'll be quicker. What d'you want?'

'Get us a Coke and that fish sandwich thing . . . '

'*Fillet-o-Fish*,' I say in a posh voice, taking the piss.

I've worked out Waj's moods and when it's OK to banter with him, and when it's most definitely fucking not. He can't eat McDonald's 'cause he's Muslim, but he goes for the fish thing to try and get round it.

'Just get my food,' he says, smiling and handing me a fifty. 'And you can keep your CD.' He ejects it and chucks the disc on the back seat, before putting in a new one – more American shit. 'Now that's more like it . . . '

I go inside and there's this fat girl serving, blonde with pigtails, and I recognise her from school. She's called Tori. Her hands are covered in Asian gold, like Ish wears. Rumour has it she stopped going out with white boys after the last one she went with bummed her. I have no idea why any lad, white or Asian, would be up for it with her.

'Can I get two large Cokes, two cheeseburgers and, erm, one Fillet-o-Fish sandwich . . . '

'*Two . . . large . . . Cokes . . .* ' she says, typing it in. She looks up at me, her face blank. 'Owt else?'

'Please,' I say. 'The two cheeseburgers, and one Fillet-o-Fish . . . '

'*Two . . . cheeseburgers . . .* ' she says, typing it in again. 'Owt else?'

'Yeah,' I say, smiling. I look down at her blouse. She's not even got any stars. 'One Fillet-o-Fish sandwich, please.'

I wait while she fetches the food.

'I'm sorry but the drinks machine is out of order. Can I get you a different beverage?'

'You got a bottle o' vodka back there, love?' I say, laughing. 'I could do wi' a drink. You could and all I bet.'

She just stares at me.

'No sorry, we don't do alcoholic beverages . . . '

I get back in the car and Waj drives up Crown Point, which isn't far, but I've already eaten my cheeseburgers by the time we pull into the car park.

You can see for miles from Crown Point, across the motorway to Accy sometimes, but it's a pretty scary place at night. There are these two car parks, one at the summit and a smaller one lower down. We come here a lot to sit and listen to music, get high. Well me, Ish and Asif do – Waj doesn't touch the stuff, just bangs on about all his old music, how you need to know that to get what's happening today. We're usually too fucked to care by then, though.

On any night there are two or three cars, one fella in each, usually smoking a fag, and they just sit there, proper dodgy. Waj thinks they're paedos but couples come up here to shag, so I reckon they're just pervs who get off watching a car get all steamed up.

Once, Waj made a point of driving up right next to one. He pulled out the car park, so Waj decided to follow. Then, for some reason, he stopped at the next car park and waited to see if we'd pass, but Waj just pulled in behind, so the car drove back to the top car park. We carried this on for about an hour and it was fucking well funny – probably 'cause we were all so high, to be fair.

I sit back in the car, relaxing as Waj eats his food, and start to think about summat he told me the other day.

'I'm making money from other people's misery,' he said, straight-faced.

I didn't say owt at the time, but I don't agree. Drugs make life worth living. There's a downside, don't get me wrong, but when you're up everything's better. It's like the time when we followed that bloke. When you're fucked, owt can be funny. There's no denying it.

The upside's not bad either. I'm earning more money than my dad has in his whole fucking life, but I'm not doing it to buy clothes and that, or to let him sit on his arse while I go school and pay the bills on top. Fuck no, I'm doing it for a different reason. I'm doing it for my mum.

I just need a bit more time.

Hayley

'She's proper annoying, though, 'cause I called her incompetent and she said I only used that word, y'know, 'cause you've been giving me extra lessons, then she called me a swot but I bet she'd soon change her tune if she knew the truth . . . don't you think, sir?'

Mr Mitchell stops kissing my neck and sits up in the driver's seat. We've been out again and are parked up Crown Point. He told me he's bored of pretending to be my dad – when we're out, so it doesn't look dodgy – then he drove us here as soon as we were finished. Nobody ever comes up Crown Point, apart from doggers.

'Actually no,' he says, panicking. 'I don't think it *would* be funny. Not funny at all.'

117

'Don't be silly, sir . . . ' I say, woozy. I think I've had too much wine. I'd not eaten all day either, before we went out, 'cause I wanted to look thin in the new dress he bought me. 'I'm only jokin'. She won't find out.' I lean over to kiss him on the cheek, but I miss and get his ear.

'And I'd rather you didn't call me that,' he says, mardy and staring straight ahead. He doesn't seem drunk at all and I can't believe I let myself get this bad. 'I'm not your teacher anymore.' He glances at me. I try to focus and give him the sexy eyes, pouting, my lips parted a bit. I'm wearing my new Bourjois lip gloss I got from Boots, 'specially for him.

It must've worked because out of nowhere he pulls me towards him, putting my hand on his thigh. I start to move it away, though, 'cause all I feel is drunk, but he keeps putting it back. He's holding my head and kissing me, shoving his tongue down my throat, and I start to feel weak, like my arms and legs are empty or made of rubber – I can't explain it. He pulls away and we stare at each other for a bit, me out of breath. Then, he unzips his trousers, and pulls me towards him again.

After he's done, he drives me home in silence. I've never done that before and wasn't really sure what I was doing. It wasn't as big as I'd expected – not even as big as my hand – and I didn't like it when he did it in my mouth, forcing my head down so I was nearly sick.

I just hope it was worth it.

CHAPTER FIFTEEN

Russell

I've just found out that my mum's suicidal.

After she hung up on Jason, she told me that she'd seriously considered killing herself 'maybe three times this year'. I asked why she could only say 'maybe three times' and not be definite about it. It's not exactly something to be unsure about, is it.

She takes pills, anti-depressants, and said that she'd thought about taking the whole pack but then chickened out, because someone told her that they can use a stomach pump on you. It sounds like she's waiting for the right time, the perfect way to do it. People say that anyone who's talking about it isn't serious. If they were, they'd just do it. This is what they call 'a cry for help'.

But what those people don't understand is, well, it's the threat that matters. She's still my mum.

This all started because I've been telling her that I want to get out of here – maybe to university, I'm not sure – and now what Jason said has made it worse. She keeps telling me that there's no point, that if I get a degree I probably won't get a job anywhere, and that I'll just end up a waste of space like my dad.

She knows that upsets me. I don't want to be like him. Not only did he leave us, he gave me this stupid name. I also think that he must be a bit of a balloon because Mum said he was suicidal too, and even tried to kill himself on the day Princess Diana died.

So, because of her depression, I've stopped wanting to argue about it. She starts crying and pleads with me not to leave her. We've reached a point where, during one of these arguments, I can't get a word in and also, if it's over the phone, I can't even end the call. *That I've made.* She just keeps me on the phone and if I do pluck up the courage to hang up she just calls and calls and calls. When she finally stops – and this is assuming I've not given in and answered – I start to picture all these melancholic scenarios in my head.

She's jumping off the multi-storey car park.

She's throwing herself in front of a train.

She's slowly slipping into a hot bath, candles around the sides and razor blades placed neatly at arm's length, Joy Division on full blast.

I know that it's a cliché, especially the last one, and that all of this probably says more about the way my mind works – the way that I can get carried away sometimes – than anything else. But knowing that doesn't make it any easier.

Like I said, she's still my mum. No matter what.

Charlie

I'm getting a haircut in the Asian barber's near mine. They always shave it too close but everyone's cool with me and it's free, 'cause of Waj and that.

The lad who's doing it doesn't look like he's from round 'ere. His hair's cropped short but he has loads of length on top, and it's all stuck up. He's wearing a low-cut V-neck T-shirt and, unlike a lot of Asians, he has a smooth chest. I can see part of a tattoo, on his right shoulder. His arms are covered in other colourful tattoos, and he has 'L.O.V.E.' on the fingers of his left hand, above and below his second knuckles. He doesn't have 'H.A.T.E.' on his other hand, though.

'D'you live near 'ere mate?' I ask as he's tidying up my neck.

'Ooh no,' he says, camp as Christmas. 'This is my uncle's place. I live in London. I'm just visiting for a few weeks and said I'd help out.'

I smile at him in the mirror. There's only one gay bar in town, the Garden Bar, and it's full of old men anyway. He's best off in London I reckon. I've heard they're all queers down there.

It's proper warm outside and finally feels like summer. We don't really get much of one, but it's a different place round 'ere when the sun's out. It's not tropical or owt but at least it's not raining and, on a day like this, when the sun's shining, people are outside and enjoying themselves, all mixing together.

These two Asian lads – wearing trackies and no tops, proper weedy – walk past me and nod. I don't know them, but I nod back anyway. Across the street there are these others unloading a van full of fresh fruit, and they recognise me. I cross and shake hands with them all, then end up going away with pockets full of apples and oranges, even a big fuck off slab of watermelon.

No idea what I'll do with that, but I suppose I can share it with Mum or summat. She'll like that.

Hayley

I'm doing some shopping for Dad 'cause we don't have owt in. He's been working so much lately and hasn't had time to pop to Asda.

It's hot today but not too hot, y'know, nice for walking about. It doesn't even matter that most places are closed, or the only ones open are takeaways and sex shops. There are loads round 'ere. Dad says there didn't used to be, but ever since I can remember it's been this way.

I walk past the Paki offy, the one what marks everything up. Dad told me to try the other one 'cause it's cheaper. Some lads start staring at me as I pass, probably 'cause I'm wearing shorts and have just put fake tan on my legs. They don't see a lot of skin I suppose, unless they're married.

Across the street there are these others unloading a van full of fresh fruit and for some reason I wink at them – then I crash right back down to earth 'cause I end up walking into Charlie, and knocking a massive watermelon out of his hands. It smashes on the pavement in front of us, splashing all over the Mini Uggs Mr Mitchell bought me.

'Oh my God I'm so sorry!' It's like I can't stop bumping into him. 'I wasn't lookin' where I was goin' . . . '

'As if,' he says, laughing. 'It was my fault. I should've been lookin' where I was goin', carryin' this watermelon like . . . I dunno . . . ' He laughs again then I laugh, so we're laughing together. It's nice.

Charlie looks really fit today. He must've had his hair cut 'cause it's really short, maybe too short at the sides but still nice, and he looks all fresh and clean and manly.

'So . . . ' I say, not wanting the moment to end. Jenny Catlow warned me but what if he likes me? I mean, what can *she* do about it? Nowt, that's what.

'So,' he says, smiling. I smile back and he laughs, I think nervously.

'What you up to later?' I blurt out, before realising how desperate I sound. 'I mean, are you doin' owt . . . tonight?'

'Erm . . . a few us were just goin' cinema, but – '

'Oh I love watching films! What are you goin' t' see? Owt good?'

'Well it's really just us lads to be honest, so . . . '

'I don't mind! I mean, if you don't . . . ?' I'm close enough to smell his aftershave and he smells really nice, not like Mr Mitchell, who smells like a dad, not *my* dad but, y'know, Kouros or Jazz, summat old fashioned like that.

'We'll probably get there round seven, go for a drink first and that . . . '

'See you then! Erm . . . *then* . . . ' I smile, not sure he gets my joke.

'Reet then Hayley,' he says, shaking his head. 'In a bit, I suppose.' He smiles and walks away.

'In a bit,' I say, trying to play it cool, even though I'm actually wanting to jump for joy and scream out 'Yippee!' right there in the middle of the street.

CHAPTER SIXTEEN

Russell

I got a text from Jason. He said that I should talk to Mum about going to college in Leeds when she's had a chance to think about it, but not to push her. After I got the text, though, I went straight down to the library to look at it online.

I go to the library a lot, but when I turned up today it was shut and there was a sign saying *CLOSED UNTIL FURTHER NOTICE*. Jason said that he'd get them to send me a prospectus with all the information, so I suppose that'll have to do. I'll just have to make sure Mum doesn't get to the post before I do over the next few days.

It was sunny when I set off to the library, but it'd started raining hard by the time I got there, so I ended up hiding in the multi-storey car park, waiting for it to pass before going back to the bus station.

For some reason I found myself going up to the top level. I couldn't help it. There were no cars and, even though it was raining, I just stood there, looking over the wall across town and letting the rain soak me.

I started to think, as I climbed the wall and sat on it, my legs dangling over the edge, who'd care if I threw myself off right now?

Would my mum? Maybe for a while, but she'd soon forget me and worry about herself as usual. She'd probably

124

just get some new pills for it anyway, rather than bother mourning me.

What about Jason? I know that he cares about me but we're barely even related. Would he be *that* upset?

The rain was streaming down my face by now, mixing in with the tears. I'm in love with the idea of love, I was thinking, but I've never actually been *in love*.

That's not true, I suppose. I loved you.

Or maybe I only love you now that you're gone. That probably doesn't count then, does it? Especially now I've stopped writing you letters. I can't help it, though. Hayley hardly knows I exist, I realise that, but it's better than writing to someone who's not even here.

Do you care anyway? And if it was the other way around, would you cry, even though I didn't when they told me about you?

I sat there, all of this going through my head, until a crowd had gathered on the ground below. Some people were calling up to me. I thought that I heard someone say 'Stop wasting our time and do it!' – but maybe it was just my imagination.

Then there was this man standing nearby, and he was calling out to me. 'Everything's going to be OK, son,' he said.

He had a kind face and a beard, and I didn't want to tell him that it wasn't what it looked like.

'I can't cope with *me*,' I said, thinking that he'd understand. 'How am I supposed to cope with everyone else?'

He just smiled, though, so I smiled back. Then I climbed down.

Charlie

I was supposed to be going for a few drinks tonight, maybe to watch a film and all, but Waj said he had some business to sort out then Hayley ended up inviting herself along, and it all got a bit out of hand.

I chucked on some jeans and a shirt Waj bought me. He had a go at me again the other day, about money. I wanted to tell him I'd been saving up to give it all to my mum, but thought better of it. He's always buying me stuff anyway but I just said there wasn't owt I liked, so he took me shopping and made me choose all this new stuff I don't even need.

We ended up waiting round in front of the pub, 'cause Hayley arrived about ten minutes late. They love to keep you waiting, girls. She was dressed in white jeans and the same Ugg boots she'd had on earlier. I don't think much of that look, but Ish told me later he reckoned she looked well fit and definitely would. Whatever.

'D'you wanna drink before we go in? I've checked and there's nowt on for about half an hour . . . '

'Yeah OK!' she said, reet enthusiastic.

We went inside and there was no one about, just a few lads who looked under-age. Ish and Asif messed about on the bandit and I went to the bar.

'What d'you want?' I asked.

'Half a lager,' she answered, smiling. I'd expected her to say a Coke or summat. Nevermind, I thought.

We sat down near the window and didn't say owt for about five minutes.

'What kind of music d'you like then?' I asked, just for

the sake of it.

'I dunno . . . ' she said, looking like I'd asked her a proper difficult question, which she didn't know the answer to but thought she should.

'Don't worry,' I said. 'What kind of question was that?' I laughed to myself and she smiled, relaxing a bit. 'What d'you wanna see then? There's that one wi' what's his face . . . erm, Keanu Reeves . . . and one wi' Will Ferrell that looks funny – '

'I 'ate comedies,' she said. I must've frowned 'cause she went all stiff. 'I mean, I don't like films what are meant to be funny, y'know?'

'Keanu Reeves it is then,' I said, looking round the bar.

What a nightmare. Ish and Asif must've reckoned we were on a date or summat, 'cause I was stuck with her all night. She's so thick, though, it's not even funny. And she's not sweet with it either, like some lasses are. I once went out with a bird, Donna, and even though she was thick as pig shit at least she was a laugh. She had a wicked sense of humour, and that counts for a lot.

Hayley, on the other hand, is a wannabe. All she talked about before the film was how she wanted to be famous. She didn't mention singing or acting or owt like that. Nah, she just wanted to be famous.

I couldn't wait to go and watch the film so we didn't have to talk. It turned out to be rubbish, course, but then again it was her choice 'cause she doesn't like comedies. What kind of person doesn't like comedies anyway. Nuff said I reckon.

I tried to get rid of her after the film but she didn't get

the message, and we ended up going into town. At least we can get pissed, I remember thinking, but the night didn't get any better. We went to Genesis and I had to introduce her to people, to be nice and that, but I bet everyone thought she was my bird.

All in all, a pretty fucking disastrous night – and that was just the start of it.

Hayley

I went out with Charlie tonight. It didn't get off to the best of starts 'cause he was with his two Paki mates, and we just sat there in silence for two hours watching the most boring film in the world ever.

I suppose that's what happens in a cinema and it was my fault for suggesting the film anyway. I'd told him I don't like comedies, pulling my face when he'd suggested one. He must've thought I was a right miserable cow.

He looked nice, though. He was wearing dark jeans and a white shirt what looked really crisp and new, like he'd just bought it and really wanted to make an effort.

We walked down into town after the film had finished and it'd only just started to go dark. Then we went to Genesis, and Charlie seemed to know everyone in there and spent time talking to all these different people, older lads I didn't recognise. When we sat down we had a table all to ourselves and the blokes behind the bar sent us over a free bottle of champagne and everything.

We didn't talk much, probably 'cause the music was so loud, but Charlie tried to shout some things in my ear and I just laughed along – I was so nervous.

After a bit Charlie said he should put me in a taxi, even though the club was still open, but I think it was 'cause he wanted me to get home safe. He's really sweet, and nowt like other boys my age.

Then, when we went outside there was this fight going on down a side street near Planet Pizza, and Charlie rushed to break it up. These two lads were beating up an old man, but Charlie wasn't scared and chased them off.

I walked over, when I could see it was just Charlie and the man, then summat weird happened. Charlie was crouched over the man, who'd been beaten up proper bad and was all bloody, and he was holding his head and stroking his hair. The man said, 'I know you don't I, love?' and Charlie nodded. I had no idea how Charlie knew this old man and why he'd said 'love' to him like that. He looked like a poof.

Anyway, we waited a while until an ambulance came, and I said I'd go with them even though Charlie said I should just get a taxi. When I did eventually get one, at A&E, I said maybe we should do it again sometime and cringed at how cheesy I sounded but he laughed, maybe thinking I was being jokey, and said we should. He actually used the word 'definitely', I think.

All in all, a perfect first date – and I didn't think of Mr Mitchell once.

CHAPTER SEVENTEEN

Russell

I've been spying on Mr Mitchell for two hours now. It wasn't meant to be this way.

I'm in Towneley Park. It's a Saturday afternoon and a nice, sunny day. The park's busy, families are lying on the grass, kids are playing football and dogs are excitedly leaping at their feet.

I just needed to get out of the house. Mum's in bed and refusing to get up because she found my prospectus, from that college in Leeds. I'd intercepted the postman the other day, so it was my fault for leaving it in my room like that. She told me that she saw it yesterday, when she was tidying.

I believed her, until she'd used the word 'tidying'.

'Leave me, Russell, go on and leave me, just like your dad, and you see what happens,' she'd said, not looking at me when I went into her bedroom this morning to give her a cup of tea.

So I came straight here, cycling all the way up the hill even though the bus goes right past.

I'd only been in the park for half an hour and was beginning to get bored. I'd not brought a book because I was in such a hurry just to get out of the house, but I'd managed to find a bench and sat there quietly, staring off into the distance.

Then he'd appeared, out of nowhere. He was on his own

by the ice cream van, holding two 99 cones. He walked right past me and towards the Hall.

After a moment, I grabbed my bike and rode after him. I don't really know why – I just couldn't help myself. He walked behind the Hall and towards the woods, right across the grass, making a beeline for them, but I followed on the bike track, keeping my distance so he didn't see me. If there's one thing I'm good at, it's not being noticed.

The woods were quiet. With the shade, I suppose on a day like this it's better to be on the grass, in the sun. I didn't know why he was walking in the woods alone, but then I saw that he was still holding the two ice creams. He must be meeting someone here in the woods, I decided. I didn't need to think hard about who that might be.

But I was wrong. Mr Mitchell *was* meeting someone, a girl, but it wasn't who I expected.

I've been here for two hours now, crouched down behind a huge rock. A boulder, actually, like the one they used to shut Jesus in his tomb. Well, according to those Roy Castle programmes they showed us at primary school.

I'm watching Mr Mitchell and a blonde girl I don't recognise. She's quite young – maybe just a bit older than me. I can't hear much, from where I'm crouched down, but I can see them. They're just talking, but look close. I can't believe it. I was sure he was seeing Hayley, but it turns out he's got a different schoolgirl lover.

Standing here, hiding behind a tree, I realise that I need to see Hayley, face to face. I need to see her before Mr Mitchell makes a fool of her and before she finds out for herself. I need to see her before she gets hurt.

131

I couldn't help you – I understand that now – but I can help Hayley.

I start to look for a way out. My bike's behind a log about twenty metres away, but I'm worried that if I stand up now they might see me.

Then I have an idea. A moment of inspiration. I watch a squirrel scurry past my feet and up a tree. Mimicking the squirrel, I get down on my front and crawl to a nearby tree then, slowly, get to my feet. I'm behind the tree now and, from where I'm standing, I can see my bike. If I do the same, just a few more times, I'll be free.

It's in this beautiful moment, when escape is within my grasp, I hear a phone ringing. The sound is unmistakeable. It's my ring-tone, the theme from *Dr. Who*, and now I'm rummaging through my pockets, desperately trying to stop the raucous ringing.

It's not long before I realise that, although it *is* my phone, my phone isn't in my pocket, and the sound is actually coming from the boulder.

I stand behind the tree, within touching distance of Mr Mitchell, and wait for it to stop.

Charlie

I've gone to the hospital to check on Roger. He got bashed pretty bad last night by some lads and I want to see if he's OK. That, and if he can remember owt about them. I'm planning on paying them a visit.

His bed's in an outbuilding and it takes me ages to find the right place. Everything's locked and there's hardly anyone about.

I hate visiting people in hospital. You go in feeling OK but as soon as you see all those sick people, and there's that smell, suddenly you're not so sure.

I find him on a ward with a load of pensioners. I suppose he's old really – I think he's about fifty – but he doesn't act it.

He sees me approach and waves. 'Well look what the cat dragged in . . . ' he says, trying to wink. His face is really bruised but they've cleared all the blood away. He doesn't look as bad as he did last night, that's for sure.

'Nice pyjamas.'

'Don't start,' he says, acting tough, like he does. 'I might look soft but I could take you young man . . . '

'What happened last night?'

'Well that was different,' he says. 'There were two of *them* – '

'Don't fuck about, Rog,' I say, interrupting again. 'Be serious for a minute.'

There's an awkward silence and I feel bad for having a go.

'Here, I brought you some grapes,' I say. 'And the stuff you asked for and all. Toothbrush, shaving foam, razor . . . even some undies and socks.' I smile at him.

'That's the least you could do,' he says, pouting and looking hard done by. I know he's joking. He's well camp and that's just his sense of humour. 'I might let you have one,' he carries on. 'A grape, that is . . . ' He smiles.

'Can you remember owt about those lads?' I ask, sitting down on a chair by the window. There's an old man in the next bed and he's moaning and groaning.

'Can you remember *anything*, you mean. Not *owt* . . .'

It pisses me off when he corrects me like that. Just 'cause he went to a posh school down south. If you're from round 'ere, you have an accent. End of.

'No, I don't remember anything about them.'

Two nurses come to the next bed and draw the curtain. There's more moaning and groaning and I glance at Roger.

'He's having a baby,' he whispers, smiling. I stand up and sit on the side of his bed, then put my hand on his.

'I know you're lyin',' I say, my voice low. 'Just tell me the truth, Rog.'

Roger looks at me until tears fill his eyes, then looks away. He acts tough, but he's not. I don't mean that in a physical way – he wouldn't hurt a fly and couldn't if he tried, soft fucker – but this kind of thing really gets to him. He lost his partner Graham, back when they lived together. Some lads jumped him right outside their flat, kicking the shit out of him when he was on the ground and stamping on his head. Roger's alone now 'cause he's never wanted to get that close to anyone again, he says. Fat lot of good it's done him and all.

I said I'd met Roger after leaving home. I'd had a fight with my dad. He'd threatened Mum and I'd got in the way, taking a bit of a beating. It was back when Dad lost his job, and the first time he'd been rough with us.

I wasn't serious, I don't think, 'cause I'd only got as far as Blackburn before I'd run out of money and ended up thumbin' a lift by the side of the motorway. Roger picked me up and, when he was driving me home, I started to cry my eyes out.

He didn't really say owt, or tell me everything'd be OK. Instead, he just drove me to this café and bought me hot chocolate. It was good just being with someone, someone who wasn't going to tell me what to do. He told me all about his life, about being gay and what that was like, for him, then he told me about Graham.

Listening to him go on, I realised something. No matter how bad I felt, it could be worse.

Hayley

I heard summat on *North West Tonight* and it made me cry.

It was Gordon Burns, and he said about six million people in Britain live alone, before going off to some sad loner in Wigan. I was only watching the news to find out about that body they found yesterday. That's the third one, and they still don't know who's doing it.

That's awful, I thought – the loner in Wigan, I mean. I hate being alone even for a night, and can't imagine living on my own. But this man in Wigan, he was a widower, about forty, and just like Dad except he didn't have kids. Dad only has me, though, and that won't be forever. I'll move out one day. I don't want to be stuck round 'ere forever.

I can still worry about him, can't I. He says he doesn't want to meet anyone else, after Mum, and it breaks my heart. I don't really want him to replace her either, but I suppose that's just me being selfish. I dunno. Sometimes I think I should just stay with him, forget school and get a job doing owt, and look after him for a change.

Still, I know he misses Mum and he'd be happier with

someone, a companion or summat. I know I would, if I were in his shoes.

I haven't seen Mr Mitchell all week. I've been going off him since that night up Crown Point, but also after my first date with Charlie.

He even asked me the other day if I'd met someone else. It's funny really, 'cause he asked me in a text, but when I got it I didn't recognise the number. It just said:

Have u met sum1 else? ;) x

I proper hate it when old people use smiley faces and reckon anyone over eighteen shouldn't be allowed to text at all.

But it made me think of that text from before, the mystery one. If it wasn't Mr Mitchell, who was it?

I realised something when I got his message. I'm bored. It was fun at first and I needed to do well in my exams, but he told me I didn't have owt to worry about. Now the excitement's gone, and he only wants one thing. I thought someone older would be more mature, but I'm getting fed up of saying no. I'd rather go out with someone independent, not desperate. Someone who's worth the chase.

Someone like, Charlie.

CHAPTER EIGHTEEN

Russell

The phone stopped ringing after a few seconds and, after waiting for a moment, I dared to look from behind the tree. It was OK, though – they'd gone – so I walked over to the boulder and found my phone lying on the ground. Then I sat down, and started to think about what I should do next.

I'm still thinking, as the bus climbs Manchester Road. I know that I need to meet Hayley and tell her what I've just seen, but I don't want her to hate me. She'll probably be really upset, and I'll have to console her.

Having said that, she might not believe what I'm saying and end up punching me or something. Girls are unpredictable like that, especially the nice ones.

The bus passes that lay-by where the first body was found. There are vans and crowds of people standing around with cameras and microphones. They look like the reporters you see on the proper news, not the ones from round here. There must have been some new information, I think, but I've not heard anything since yesterday.

My mind wanders back to Hayley, and how she'll react. She might be angry but I suppose I can't control that really. I'll just have to wait and see.

Charlie

I'm in Waj's car, thinking about what I'm about to do.

Roger told me what I wanted to know, eventually, and I couldn't believe it. I'd not been able to make them out on the night 'cause it was so dark and, by the time I'd got to him, they'd fucked off. But now I know.

'Why are we here?' says Waj, turning the music down for a minute. 'I still don't understand why you asked me to drive you – '

'It's nowt,' I interrupt. 'Will you wait for us, though? I've just got summat I . . . I need to take care of. It won't take long . . . ' I get out the car but Waj grabs my arm.

'Should I come with?' he asks, still gripping me.

'No, I'll be reet. Just wait here.'

'OK,' he says, his eyes fixed on mine. 'But don't make me wait too long. I've got something I need to talk to you about.'

I walk through town, past the boarded up precinct where all the crackheads hang about. They're sitting round a fountain put in by the Council a few years ago. I've stopped being able to recognise them and feel a bit bad for it, but if I'm honest they've all started to look the same. Apart from the ones who are trouble, course. Forget being sensitive. You'd be a thick cunt to forget those faces. You never know when they might jump you.

The snooker club's between a launderette and a flea market, under the culvert and up Stanton Street. I've told Waj to meet me at the top of the road opposite TK Maxx, 'cause of the one-way system and that. It's quiet most nights of the week, but I know they'll be here 'cause I got a tip off from a lad I do a lot of business with who works the door. He's a bouncer at Genesis, and a good bloke to know if you're up to no good and don't want to be disturbed. He's sorted it so nobody's about when I turn up.

I walk upstairs and into the main room on the top floor. I can hear them already, messing round and talking shit. Some snooker cues are lined up at the top of the stairs, where I'm standing, but I don't need them. I've already brought my weapon of choice. It's a club from when we used to go causing trouble after the football. We'd get into scraps with other fans, the three of us, 'specially after games against Preston.

Ironic, really, seein' as I'm about to use it to bash them now.

Hayley

Dad's working lates again tonight but left us some money, so it's just me, lying in bed watching telly while stuffing my face with a Domino's. I shouldn't really, but I don't know how to make owt slimming.

Mum used to say, 'One day your metabolism'll slow down and that milkshake'll go straight to your bum.' We'd always go to this café in the precinct, and they did the best milkshakes – ones with a big dollop of ice cream on top. 'Until then, stuff your face like crazy!'

I miss Mum when I'm on my own. It used to be that Dad'd be out working and Mum and me would stay up, just watching the box and waiting for him to come home.

There's summat on the news about those murders. It's on the proper news channel, not just the local one. Apparently the men were gang leaders, and all white. They think it's the Pakis what are doing it, and now there are reporters standing about on streets round 'ere – near that lay-by, or in the roughest parts of town. They say it's not been this bad since the riots, but I was only little then so can't really remember.

I get up and look out the window, thinking I can hear summat. There was a helicopter above our house earlier, but nowt now.

Then my phone vibrates, and I grab it from under the pillow. I have a text, from that mystery number:

Please will you meet me?

I don't get it and am about to text Mr Mitchell, asking why he's sending me messages from a weird number, but then I stop.

It might be him. I know he wants to see me, and I know just why. But what if it's not Mr Mitchell at all, and I was right the first time?

It's from Charlie, it has to be. He said he wanted to see me again. He even used the word 'definitely', I'm sure.

'Apply yourself Hayley my girl,' Mum once said to me, when she knew she only had a little bit of time left. 'Earn your rewards. You only get out what you put in.'

I never really understood what she was getting at, but maybe she meant I should take a risk, y'know, a chance – and see what happens.

Well, I suppose there's only one way to find out.

CHAPTER NINETEEN

Russell

I suppose this is goodbye then.

I'm at home in my room, writing to you for the very last time. I've been doing this once a week for three years – not just letters, but poems too.

You would've been sixteen today, and I would've written something special in your card. You would've laughed at me, like you did when I wrote you that poem – the first love letter I ever wrote for anyone, and the first you'd ever received. I would've expected it, though.

I even tried writing you a song. Do you remember that? I played it on my Bontempi keyboard. I couldn't read music – I still can't – so my mum used to have to learn the song herself, then write down the keys I needed to press, giving each one a number. 'Silent Night' started with '5-6-5-3' and every time I hear it, I think about my Bontempi keyboard, and writing a song for you.

But enough's enough. It doesn't feel right, not now someone else needs help, someone who's actually here, with me. I was too late to help you, but I can make up for that now.

You know how I feel about you, don't you? I think you always did. I didn't exactly hide it, did I.

What is love?

I've thought about the answer to that question so many times. The truth is, though, love isn't an overbearing and burdensome weight. It shouldn't be so hard that you forget why, and just focus on the pain. It shouldn't be a burden that you have to bear alone. It shouldn't make you sad, or else it's not real love.

I'll miss you.

Charlie

I get back in the car and wipe my hands on the dashboard. I have blood on them, my head's spinning and I really need to calm the fuck down.

'Pass us that, Waj . . . ' I say to him, pointing at what's left of the weed.

He hands it me and I just sit there, trying to roll a joint, my hands shaking as we drive off. Waj presses play on the CD and puts his foot down, overtaking car after car, even though we're in a thirty zone.

> *Y'know . . . we're dealin' wit' . . . a very critical*
> *and crucial time,*
> *The most . . . crucial and critical time that I have*
> *ever witnessed . . .*

I can't see owt out the window 'cause it's all steamed up, the weed's starting to make me sick, and his driving's really not fucking helping.

> *If you don't work . . . you can't eat . . .*
> *If you don't work . . . you can't eat . . .*
> *Get hip to yourself good God my brother,*
> *And get it from the street . . .*

Waj accelerates past a lorry and my head jolts back, then I start to throw up in my mouth, before swallowing, my eyes filling with tears.

'Waj pull over.'

'Just chill out, Charlie. We're nearly there . . . '

Mind power . . .

Mind . . . mind power . . .

'I think I need to go home, Waj,' I say as we pull into the car park at the summit.

'You're a tough lad, Charlie,' he says, ignoring me and switching the engine off. 'People fear you, but they also respect you.' I've closed my eyes, but can't block him out. 'I didn't fully understand that when . . . but I suppose it was the same with the Krays, so . . . ' He trails off, thinking carefully about what he wants to say. 'People fear you and they also respect you. That's why you're ready.'

'Ready for what?' I turn to face him. Brooker's battered face flashes in front of my eyes and I have to blink to get rid of the image.

'You can't have one without the other,' he says, staring straight ahead and still not listening. 'If they don't fear you, they'll fuck you and apologise afterwards. If they don't respect you, well, then you're not worth fucking are you?' He laughs, shakes his head.

'What you goin' on about?' I say. My headache's getting worse and I've closed my eyes again, but now it's Digger, holding out his hand, begging me to stop. 'I'm not feelin' too good, Waj. I think you should just drive me home.'

'OK Charlie,' I think he says, 'cause I can barely hear him, 'this can wait . . . this can wait until tomorrow . . . '

Waj drops me off on the corner of my street, and as soon as I get in I run upstairs to the bathroom and spew

143

my guts up. I don't know what's got into me. I don't give a shit about Brooker and Digger, not now.

I dry my eyes on some bog roll and sit down, my back against the door. I'm tough, remember. Feared and respected. That's what Waj just said. That's what everyone thinks.

If only they knew, I think, the tears filling up in my eyes again. If only they knew.

Hayley

I wake up in the middle of the night. I was having a nightmare again – not about Charlie, but about Mr Mitchell.

I'm following him but he doesn't know I'm there. He's on his way somewhere, I dunno, somewhere in town I think.

Then suddenly we're in a house, a bedroom, and I'm standing behind him.

'I saw you in a dream,' he says, not looking at me. It's him, but he doesn't sound himself, y'know, a bit weird, and he's standing in front of a camera.

'What was I doing?' I ask.

'You were smiling sweetly.'

'Where was I?'

'You were standing in a bedroom, like this. It was night-time, and cold. So cold . . . '

'What did I look like?'

'You looked young . . . so young . . . '

'Why was I there?'

'You were moving towards me. I was on the bed, filming you and telling you the camera loved you, and this was making you laugh. I was telling you I loved you. You were telling me you loved me, too. I was telling you not to say "too". You looked so young . . . '

'Then what happened?'

'You asked me to turn the camera off. I moved towards you, still filming. You tried to move away but I stopped you and took off your dress.'

He turns round and comes over to me, like he wants to kiss me.

But before it can happen everything changes and I'm in a club, dancing on my own.

Well I think I'm on my own, but then I see Mr Mitchell and he's leading a girl, a girl who looks like the waitress from that Italian restaurant, through a door at the back of the club. Before he walks through the door he looks back at me, and smiles.

I try to go after them but a big bouncer stops me at the door, and tells me I can't go there, I'm not allowed, it's not OK, and I'm screaming at him and telling him I *am* allowed, I know Mr Mitchell, and he'll want me to, but the bouncer doesn't let me past.

That's all I remember, though, 'cause that's when I wake up, still screaming my head off so loud Dad actually comes into my room. I don't tell him about the nightmare but just hug him, crying into his arms.

And he doesn't speak, just holds me, stroking my hair until I drift off back to sleep.

CHAPTER TWENTY

Russell

This lad shouts 'Polish tramp!' at an old man while he's getting on the bus. The old man, who's brown and dressed in a fawn suit, is walking away towards TJ Hughes. Fawn, I think as I watch him, looking sad and dejected. An insipid, decrepit shade of nothingness that's popular in the north of England. Quite appropriate really.

The old man must've really upset this lad, who's dressed in an oversized white Lacoste jumper, black tracksuit pants and scuffed Reebok Classics. He's clearly wound up, like he wants to hit someone, so I look away as he walks past me to the back of the bus.

I'm on the X43. I had to pick up something for my mum from Ethel Austin in Rawtenstall, because they didn't have it in the one in town. The X43 goes through there. Well, it goes through everywhere to be honest. The bus takes forever because it goes around the houses and picks up anyone and everyone. Old biddies, school kids – anyone and everyone. It's got leather seats, though, so it's not all bad.

I've never actually been to Manchester before, even though it's not that far. I've always wanted to, but I've never had anybody to go with. I love going to Leeds because, there, being different isn't about listening to metal in your bedroom or, if you're really brave, dying your hair a funny colour, like it is where I'm from. In cities like Leeds and Manchester, nobody looks at you funny or beats you up for being different – because there's always someone who's more different than you. You can just get on with being yourself.

As we come over the tops from Rawtenstall, a young mum gets on pushing a pram and with another kid in tow. She looks about my age and is wearing fake Ugg boots. She's got a pretty face but, unless the dad's around, which I bet he's not, what use is that to her now. That was probably the trouble in the first place.

My MP3 player runs out of battery so I pick up a *Sun* from the seat next to me. The front three pages are all about those murders. They've identified the bodies and the paper's linking what's happening now to the race riots, from years ago. The whole world's got something to say about it, and all these politicians are suddenly interested – with each side blaming the BNP, immigration, or each other. The article says that the murders are down to 'racial tensions in the area'. I'm not sure why it took them so long to come to that conclusion, because everyone knows that's exactly what it's all about. It's nothing new.

Anyway, the police have 'a lead in the Asian community' – the paper even has a fuzzy image of someone who might be able to identify the murderers. You can't really tell much from the photo, though. It could be anyone.

I throw the paper aside and look out of the window, between the trees, trying to spot the mansion where that Premiership footballer lives. I don't know why a famous footballer would want to live here. As soon as I got what my mum wanted in Ethel Austin, I turned around and went straight back to the bus station. There was this sign that said *Probably the Friendliest Market in the World* and I thought, standing in front of it and waiting for the bus to turn up, maybe they're being ironic.

But then there were also these two tramps nearby, and they were dancing to imaginary music and swigging cans of Special Brew. I was listening to 'Just Can't Get Enough' by Depeche Mode and it was almost as if they were dancing to that, so I smiled at them and they smiled back and signalled 'cheers' with their cans.

My phone buzzes, and I see that I've got a text. I haven't had one in ages, so am a bit surprised, but then I'm even more surprised when I see who it's from:

Where and when? Hayley xo

I text back without thinking:

Towneley Park. The woods behind the Hall. 7pm.

Then I start to panic, the message long gone, as I realise that I actually have to go through with it.

Charlie

We get our results soon and I've been thinking about what I'm doing next year. Don't get me wrong. I've been busy working for Waj and saving up enough money to make things right at home, but it's been weighin' on my mind.

My dad's lost interest to be honest, and I don't reckon he cares if I stay on. He's stopped asking where I'm getting all my money from and all – just takes his cut. I suppose he's realised it means he doesn't have to get off his arse and find a job, but he's not been speaking to me. Mum's getting it in the neck now, course, but she won't have to for long. Once that bag of money stuffed under my bed's full, she'll be free of him.

I'm at my cousin's in Clayton-le-Moors. He's having a barbecue on the street and, even though I don't see much of him 'cause he's always been a bit of knob, it's so hot today and I just wanted to get out the house.

My cousin, Lee, is a proper dole dosser and lives on a rough street in the centre of Clayton. We're having chicken, which is like charcoal, but the whole street's out and it's actually a good laugh with everyone joining in, passing cans of Stella and that round.

I don't know if it's 'cause it's hot out, but I'm always proper horny come summer. Some rough-looking birds are hanging round, mainly talking to these older lads who are all shirtless, dressed only in trackies and baseball caps. They're pale fuckers but a few of them have decent physiques. I make eye contact with one of the lads. He's got a skinhead and loads of tattoos all over his arms and back. He nods. I nod back.

The match is on and we're all sitting in Lee's front garden, which is really just a few square feet of flags. He's put the TV on top of an old Ford Escort, the extension cord stretching through the house. There's music blaring from inside – that mind-numbing happy hardcore shit – and it must look a bit daft to anyone not from round 'ere, but it's open-air theatre to us.

I keep seeing all that stuff about those murders on the news, and hearing how we're not right round 'ere – that we're the underclass and the reason Britain's broken. Well y'know what, I think, finishing my beer. Fuck 'em.

'Another one Charlie lad?' Lee says, already handing me a can. He's sitting on a deck chair, his feet on the wall. 'It's good to see you, pal . . . '

'Same 'ere,' I say, leaning back. I hate not being able to see someone when I'm talking to them, but all these people keep walking in and out the house, getting in the way.

'It's alreet round 'ere int it?' he says, trying to look at me as this fat lass walks past, mouthing off into her phone. 'Not full o' Pakis like where you live!' He laughs and takes a swig of his can.

My phone rings as I watch the skinhead mis-kick the ball, sending it rolling away down the street. He laughs, looking at me as I stand and take the phone out my pocket. He's sweaty from all the running and I watch as he fags the ball from under a parked car.

'Where d'yer get that from?' Lee asks, nodding at my iPhone, like he's never seen one before.

I look at the phone, which is still ringing. It's Waj.

'Alreet Waj,' I answer, ignoring Lee. 'One sec . . . '

I go inside the house for some peace and quiet, and find myself a bedroom.

'What's crack?'

'I've been calling you for the last three days,' he says, sounding pissed off. 'Where have you been?'

'Soz Waj. I've been a bit – '

'Where are you?' he snaps. 'I'll pick you up. I've got something I need to talk to you about.'

'I'm in Clayton-le-Moors at – '

'What are you doing in Clayton-le-Moors?' He's laughing but doesn't sound too happy about it. He sounds different – short, and a bit on edge.

'I'm at a barbecue. I'll be back in town in a – '

'Look meet me at Towneley Park,' he says, interrupting again. 'I'll be there at seven, in front of the Hall.'

As he hangs up I notice the skinhead standing in the doorway.

'Lee tells me yer can sort us out wi' stuff . . . '

'Depends,' I say, getting up from the bed and walking towards the door to leave.

'Have yer got owt on yer now?' he says, blocking the door. He's hot and sweaty, and I get a whiff of that outdoors smell on him.

'I've got a wrap and a joint . . . '

'I don't do that,' he jumps in, before looking down at his feet, embarrassed. He puts his hands down his trackies, the way scallies do. I've never understood why and I'm not about to ask now. 'But I'll share a joint wi' yer . . . ?' He looks up at me and grins.

'No probs,' I say, going over to the bed.

'Sound,' he says, nodding. 'Yer proper sound, mate.'

I light the joint and pass it him, before lying back on the bed. He takes one drag and stands over the bed, looking at me.

'Yer not hot?' he asks. 'I can't believe yer've still got yer shirt on. It's fuckin' boilin' in 'ere . . . '

'Open the window then,' I say, staring at the ceiling. 'Use your cap as a fan. Take your fuckin' trackies off for all

151

I care. But shut the fuck up . . . ' I laugh out loud, the weed hitting.

'Yer mental!' he says, laughing and all. 'As if . . . '

'What?' I say, taking another big drag and closing my eyes. 'You ashamed of your tool or summat?'

I lie there, letting the beer and the weed, and the vallies I did this morning, take effect. I've been doing more drugs lately but I've got a lot going on, and it's not like they're in short supply round 'ere, 'specially for me.

I'm getting high but then realise the lad hasn't said owt for a bit, so sit up.

'How's this for ashamed?' he says.

He's standing there naked except for his cap, which is hanging off his knob. He moves the cap up and down with his hardon, and I just burst out laughing. It's the funniest thing I've ever seen.

'Fuck, I best close the door,' he carries on, shutting it then turning the key in the lock. 'Don't want anyone disturbin' us do we . . . '

Hayley

I get to the park just before seven but I'm a bit lost, and I don't really know where I'm going. The text just said the woods, behind the Hall. When I get to the Hall, though, I see a black X5 parked outside and panic. I recognise the tinted windows but I can't make out the driver.

Then, out of nowhere, I see Charlie. I can feel myself going red, as usual, but I'm a bit relieved as well to be honest. I always knew it was him what texted me, and I'm so happy I want to jump on him.

'Hi,' I say, going over and trying not to come across too keen. 'I thought you said we should meet in the woods . . . ?'

'Erm . . . what?' he says. He looks different, I dunno, proper stressed.

'In your text, you said the woods . . . oh nevermind! Anyway . . . erm, I'm sorry I didn't text back much, earlier. I don't want you thinking I've lost interest in . . . well, y'know . . . '

'Lost interest in what?' He looks confused.

'*Us*,' I say back, frowning. 'I mean, I'd like to do it again . . . '

'Look Hayley,' he says, not looking at me. 'I, erm . . . the thing is . . . ' He trails off. 'Soz,' he says, after a moment. He's looking at me now. 'I can't do this right now.'

He walks off and gets in the X5, which skids as it drives away, covering me in dust.

CHAPTER TWENTY-ONE

Russell

I'm standing in the enclosed bit of woodland where I caught Mr Mitchell. It's nearly eight, and I've been here for an hour. Hayley's late, and I'm beginning to realise that she's not coming.

One part of me is relieved, if I'm honest. I hadn't really thought this through, I mean, what I was going to say exactly, and how I was going to put it.

Perhaps I should just leave it completely, and mind my own business – keep my head down, just like Mr Mitchell said. She doesn't know that it's me and I could just text her and say I've changed my mind. Sorry for the inconvenience and all that. I could even just not text, and after a while she'd forget all about it.

No, I need to tell her. It's not right for me to keep this to myself, and I can't let her get hurt. If she won't meet me, I'll just have to think of another way to help her.

It's starting to go dark now. I shouldn't be out here on my own, I think, so I make my way towards the Hall, and out of the woods. There's a cemetery behind it and sometimes I just like to walk around and be by myself, because it's so peaceful – but I don't want to end up there in the dark.

As I near the edge, the light at the end visible, I hear a shout from behind me.

'Oi!' the voice sounds again. 'What the fuck are *you*

doin' 'ere? This is *our* patch . . . '

I turn around and see two lads approaching. Even at this distance, I recognise them instantly.

I start to run.

Charlie

I met Waj at Towneley earlier and we went to the cemetery. It's quiet and a good place to get away from it all. I didn't want him taking me back to mine after, and I also just wanted to be on my own for a bit, so he's just dropped me off in the bus station. I'll probably walk home. I've got a lot to think about.

Waj told me he'll have to keep his head down, until all this stuff about those murders goes away and he finds out who's been talking. He says it's nowt to do with him but bad for business, the pigs and papers sniffing round.

And he wants me to stay local. He reckons he's been priming me for it, and thinks we've expanded enough to justify diversifying – his word, not mine – so he's taking on Manchester. He's got a flat there and loads of contacts and that. Anyway, all that stuff about me being ready, about being feared and respected – that was about me taking over. I'd be in charge round 'ere, which would mean sacking off school and doing this, in Waj's words, 'full-time'.

I said I've got a lot to think about.

'Oi Charlie!' I hear from behind me. I turn round and see it's Jenny. I'm walking up Manny Road, my head still a bit all over the place.

'Not now Jenny,' I say, turning round and carrying on up the road.

'What did yer do that to Brooker and Digger for?' She catches up and grabs hold of my arm, spinning me round and pushing me against the wall. I can see she's been crying, mascara all down her cheeks. 'I've bin callin' yer. Yer've 'ad me fuckin' runnin' up 'ere after yer . . . ' She trails off and bursts into tears.

'Oi,' I say, pressing her hand in mine. 'Come on, calm down . . . '

'Why dint yer tell me, Charlie?' she says, pulling her hand away, tears streaming down her face. I try to wipe them but she flinches and pulls back. 'Don't touch me!'

'What d'you mean?' I say. Jenny's always been fucking unpredictable, but this I've never seen before.

'I know, Charlie. *I know* . . . ' She falls to her knees in front of me, so I get down on mine and put my arm round her.

'Look just calm down – '

'Tell me why,' she says, pushing my arm away. She's looking right at me and suddenly sounds focused. 'Tell me why yer'd beat the shit outta Brooker and Digger. I wanna 'ear it from *you*.'

'I dunno,' I whisper, not knowing what else to say.

'Fine,' she says, standing up. 'If yer won't say it, *I will*. It's 'cause yer a queer!' She looks at me, smiling that same mad grin she had when she set fire to that body.

'Leave me alone, Jenny,' I say, already walking away, back down Manny Road.

I don't want to go home now. I just want to see Roger, and talk to him about what's happening. Jenny can wait.

'It's true int it?' she says, chasing after me until she's in my way again, walking backwards. 'They beat up that bender in town, and yer did same to them for revenge. Why else would yer bother? Them two are nowt, 'specially t' likes o' *you*. I shoulda seen it. I spoke to Lee today. He's always reckoned yer for a poof but I dint believe him. I thought yer were avoidin' us 'cause of them druggies yer've bin hangin' round wi'. But yer've bin avoidin' us, avoidin' *me*, 'cause yer like it up the arse!'

I grab hold of her wrists and push her back against the wall, hard enough for her to know I'm serious.

'Fuck off, Jenny,' I growl. 'Fuck off and die.'

I leave her there, crying against the wall, and try Roger's number. He told me he'd be out of hospital today but he can't be 'cause he would've just gone straight home, and he always answers his phone.

By the time I get back to the station I must've called ten times, so decide I should just go to the hospital again, and find out where he is. I jump on the first mainline and keep calling his house, all the time thinking of the last time I saw him, before all this happened.

I'd gone round his one morning, after getting up to find mine empty – no sign of either Mum or Dad. I was scared and called the police, but they told me I couldn't report a missing person for twenty-four hours. I tried telling them about everything, how Mum'd never disappear like that without telling me, but they didn't care.

Roger didn't mess about. He got his car and we drove about, looking for Mum in every place I could think of. We drove round and round for hours, and Rog never complained, or told me to give up. After four hours, we ended up at the crematorium out of town, where my grandma's buried. I found Mum inside the registrar's office, in her nightie and slippers. No fucker had bothered to ask what she was doing there but, thinking about it now, she probably just wanted to be somewhere safe.

I get to Roger's ward, eventually, but he's not there. No one seems to know where he is. The muppets I manage to get hold of can't find a record of him and tell me I have to see the main reception desk.

I go there next and as soon as I say his name the two receptionists look at each other funny, and after a bit an Asian doctor comes over.

He looks important, dressed in a suit, and he has this proper solemn look on his face when he asks if I'm family. I tell him Roger has no family, but I'm a close friend. The doctor seems to get this and takes me through the back into a makeshift room with one bed and one plastic chair. It's cramped, and only closed off by a curtain. He pulls it to and I start to feel cold. Then he offers me some water and I say I'm fine. I just want him to tell me where Roger is.

It's when I'm sitting there, my head spinning from every-thing, which is only made worse by the noise of other patients and nurses coming from behind the curtain, that he tells me the news.

I leave the hospital in a daze and stagger towards the main road. It's nearly dark now, and I end up back on a bus and going across town, but I get off just before the bus station, fuck knows why, and walk towards the park. I keep moving, until I get past Towneley Hall and back to the cemetery. I have nowhere else to go.

Roger was due to be discharged this morning, just after they found him in the ward's bathroom. He'd slit his wrists, according to the doctor, with the razor blade I'd brought in for him.

I'd only asked one question, which the doctor answered for me straight away.

When they found Roger, his eyes were closed.

Hayley

On my way home from the park I got a text. It wasn't from Charlie, though. It was from Mr Mitchell.

It cheered me up, in a funny way. I was having a bit of a cry, 'cause I liked Charlie and thought he was different to other boys my age. But when I got home, and thought about it for a bit up in my room, I started to realise he's just immature.

I know we had a good time together, on our date, but it feels like he's scared. I don't want to be with a *boy*, and I suppose I was a bit stupid to think he'd be different to the rest. He's only sixteen.

Mr Mitchell isn't scared, though. I know what we wants, like all men really, but I also know he's not like anyone I've ever met. He makes me feel special, when he takes me out places and we talk. He always says he likes it when I tell him about what I want to do with my life, and I feel like he's really listening. I suppose you can never tell for sure, y'know, what people are really like, deep down. I just know how he makes me feel sometimes.

Maybe that's what my mum was getting at, when she said I should take risks. Maybe I should take a chance –

not with Charlie, but with Mr Mitchell. Maybe I should just go for it, and see what happens.

I text him, and arrange to meet.

CHAPTER TWENTY-TWO

Russell

I leg it towards the cemetery and as I burst through the gates think that I just need to get across to the other side then I'll be at the main road, and I daren't look back but know that Brooker and Digger are still chasing me and can't be far behind, so I sprint as fast as I can over graves and in between tree shrines with laminated bits of cards and spinning windmills and stuff like that stuck to them, then I see the gate at the other side and realise that I'm almost there.

But then Brooker appears from nowhere, behind the gate, and I try to turn back. Now Digger's right behind me, though – he's just come through the other gate – and I'm trapped.

'I thought we warned yer,' says Digger, approaching me now.

'I, erm . . . I don't know what you mean,' I say, out of breath. My palms are sweaty but I'm freezing cold. I feel like I'm about to cry but know that, if I do, I'm dead.

'We said we dint wanna see yer outside school,' says Brooker, now standing next to me. 'And if we did, we'd do worse than chuck yer mosher boots in t' canal.'

'But I . . . ' I trail off, not sure which way to turn.

I reach into my pocket for my phone, to call the police – someone, anyone – for help. But before I can Digger punches me in the stomach, winding me, then Brooker kicks me in my side while I'm bent over, sending me stumbling.

I scramble to my feet but Brooker kicks me again, and I fall flat on my face on top of someone's grave. Then I try and stand up again, my back against the gravestone so I can see them coming for me, but I don't have the strength. I'm willing myself to my feet, but my body just won't respond.

Digger grabs me and picks me up by my shirt collar, and I lash out desperately, kicking him in the shins. I spot my chance and try to run to the nearest gate, but before I can get more than a few steps Brooker plants his fist in the side of my face, sending me sprawling head first into a tree.

'Yer fuckin' dead!' Digger shouts, looming over me. I put my hand to my lip and see that I'm bleeding.

'Fuck off!' someone yells from behind us.

Brooker and Digger jump back, and I turn around. It's Charlie.

'You not hear me?' he says, coming closer, his fists clenched. He looks terrifying. 'Or do I need to tell you twice?'

Even though there are two of them, Brooker and Digger look like they're about to start crying. They're not so tough now and run away, leaving the cemetery through the far gate.

Charlie sits on the bench, near to where I'm lying in a heap. 'That's three times I've saved your life now,' is all he says, looking down at his feet.

'Erm, thanks . . . ' I manage. I try to stand up, wiping my face. My jaw's throbbing and there's blood in my mouth.

'But I thought it was only two,' I say, spitting some blood on the grass. 'Not that I'm being ungrateful . . . '

'Yeah?' he says, still looking down at his feet. 'Think you'll find it's three. There's now, then there was that time on the bus . . . then when I rescued you from the bogs at school.'

'That was you?' I say, sitting down next to him, carefully, my right side aching. I've never broken a bone before but it feels like all my ribs are cracked and, if I press them, I'll crumple in on myself. 'I didn't know . . . '

When I was little, I went with my mum to our school Nativity play. I wasn't confident enough to be in it – not even as an extra, a donkey, or even a tree – but my mum still wanted to watch it and said that I might make more friends if I got involved in stuff like that. She's always been full of helpful advice, my mum.

Anyway, I went to the toilet in the interval and used a cubicle, because I didn't feel comfortable standing next to people. I forgot to lock the door then some lads burst in, laughing at me. So I locked it, embarrassed, but as I did I noticed a Highland Toffee wrapper wedged in the lock, then I couldn't unlock it no matter how hard I tried. I panicked, and the people in the toilets had to go and get my mum. Out of nowhere, though, a lad climbed over the cubicle wall then lifted me back over with him.

I'd always just thought that it was an older lad – I couldn't bear to look at him when I'd said thank you, I was so humiliated – but it turns out that it was Charlie, all along.

Charlie

I know what I've got to do, I think as I climb into bed, pissed, and bury my head in the pillow.

I've had so much on my mind lately. I can't sleep, my head's always spinning 'cause I've got it all going round and round, and I can't make sense of owt. But I keep thinking about what Roger always used to tell me, when I got in trouble, or a hard time from my dad.

'You're a special boy, Charlie,' he'd say, and I'd always frown, dead uncomfortable. 'Don't end up a waste of space, or you'll break my heart.'

I never got to talk to him about all this, and I know what he would've said. He hated drugs but always told me to do what I thought was best.

Now Roger's gone, and I've got nobody, it's down to me.

Truth is I never wanted to get involved with Waj, but when I met him it seemed too good to be true. I needed a way to contribute at home, and he was offering it me on a plate. But now I'm making more cash than I can fit under my bed, and it's getting ridiculous. Why would I stay on at school, just to get mugged off with a few A-Levels and no job at the end of it.

That just leaves my mum. I've got enough now to help her, then we can both get on with our lives. Away from him.

Hayley

I'm sitting in Mr Mitchell's car up Crown Point, telling him about Charlie. I'm not trying to make him jealous, but he's the only person I feel like I can talk to about this stuff. I can't talk to Gemma – she's too immature – and there's no way I can talk to Dad. He won't understand, and will only think the worst of me.

'I thought you might be seeing someone,' he says.

'I'm not . . . I mean, I was I suppose, but I'm not . . . look I don't know what I want.'

I look out the window, feeling like I'm about to cry. I'm confused and thought he'd understand, but maybe there's nobody out there who'll ever get me.

'Actually, I think I just want to go home,' I carry on, thinking this was a mistake. 'I've forgot my phone and if Dad rings me he'll be – '

'Well what about what *I* want?' he interrupts. He turns on the light above our heads.

'What d'you mean?' I say, turning round to face him. He's looking straight ahead, like he does sometimes, when he's in a big fat mood.

'You said something, when we were together last time, about not being . . . '

'Not being what?' I say, impatient.

'*Ready.*'

He turns to face me, and I know right then what I've got to do.

I creep inside after he drops me off, trying not to wake Dad as I close the front door. It's hard to see owt, but I tip-toe through the hall and into the kitchen. I'm starving and feel like I've not eaten for days.

When I open the door, Dad's waiting for me at the kitchen table.

'Oh hi Dad,' I say, actually happy to see him. I open the fridge and look for summat to nibble on. 'I didn't wake you did I? Shall I make us some tea then we can maybe watch a DVD? It's not too late is it? We've got that new one wi' Robert Pattinson and . . . ' I trail off as I realise he's not listening to me going on, and instead is just staring at summat in his hand.

'Who's this?' he says, looking up at me. 'Is this the bloke yer've bin seein'? Is this why yer never 'ome no more?' He stands up and comes over to me. I want to run out of the room, but I can't move. I'm frozen by the fridge-freezer.

He thrusts the phone, *my* phone, in front of me and I see what he's been looking at. It's a text message from Mr Mitchell of a photo he took when we were out, ages ago. He sent it me earlier, and I forgot to delete it when I went out. Mr Mitchell's kissing me in the photo.

'Daddy it's not what it looks like . . . '

'Yer must think I were born yesterday, Hayley!' He looks angrier than I've ever seen him before. 'Who is it?'

'Just someone from school,' I say, then regret it. Why would I say that? 'I mean . . . well . . . it's from a school trip, last year . . . erm, d'you remember when we went to Liverpool, for that art exhibition? Well that's – '

'Hayley I know who it is,' he interrupts again. 'I've met the bloke at a bloody parent-teacher evening!'

'Why were you looking at my phone anyway?' I say, desperate, and storming out. 'It's none of your business . . . '

'Yer left it right 'ere!' He catches me up and stands in front of the stairs, so I can't get past. 'I couldn't miss it,

166

Hayley. It were starin' me back in t' face!'

We don't say owt for a bit, then he sits down on the bottom step.

'I've a good mind to march down to that school, first thing, and knock 'is bloody 'ead off,' he says, turning to look at me. 'But then what does that meck *you* look like, eh?'

'I don't know what to say . . . '

'I dint think you would, lass,' he says, shaking his head. 'I just wanted t' know whether yer'd lie.'

He stands up to walk out the room, and doesn't look at me.

'If yer mum could see yer now . . . '

CHAPTER TWENTY-THREE

Russell

It's results day and I'm first to arrive at school.

I'm nervous as I make my way inside. It's so quiet, apart from a few teachers milling around, and there are all these envelopes lined up on a table in the assembly hall.

'Russell Crackle please,' I say, looking down at my feet, conscious of how much of a mess I look. The bruising hasn't gone and I must look really tough, even though I actually feel like I'm going to shatter into a million pieces any minute now.

I look up, after a moment, and see that it's Mr Mitchell behind the desk. I stare at him, and think about whether Charlie's seen him yet, but he doesn't look at me and just hands me my envelope.

I don't open it until I get outside and away from the main entrance, so there's no chance of interruption.

'Oh well, Russell,' I say to myself, closing my eyes. 'This is it, I suppose. The moment of truth . . . '

Charlie

It's results day and I'm last to arrive at school.

Everyone's round the main entrance, standing in the car park – some in groups, some alone talking into their phones. Jenny's there, leaning against some lad's Corsa, and blanks me as I walk past. I don't give a fuck, though.

Then I see a cop car. Waj just dropped me off and said

168

he'd wait on the main road, but when I spin round I see he's already clocked them and done one. I walk towards the doors, calm as you like, thinking about who they might be questioning, and if they're any closer to finding the grass. My hand's already on the door when a pig comes out the other, followed by another – then Ish. We don't make eye contact, and I just glide past.

Inside there's a big desk with one envelope on it. Everyone must already know what they've got. I say my name to a woman and she hands me the envelope, then I make my way out the main hall and into the corridor, opposite the staff room.

As I tear the envelope open and unfold the slip of paper inside, all computerised markings and codes, my name and student number at the top, Hayley appears. Her shirt's ripped and she looks a mess. She storms past me, then I turn round and Mr Mitchell's standing in the staff room doorway, rubbing his face. We make eye contact and he forces a smile at me, before crawling off to the staff bogs.

Russell said summat about him, in the cemetery. We talked for hours that night, about school, about stuff at home, even about girls. He told me he liked Hayley. I told him not to bother.

'You're probably right,' he said. 'It's not as if I can take her out for meals and on holidays. I'm no match for Mr Mitchell . . . '

'You what?' I said, laughing and turning to face him on the bench.

Then he told me all about Mr Mitchell, how the

rumours were true, and he was having it off with other girls and all – not just Hayley.

Russell wanted to sort Mr Mitchell, but couldn't. Thing is, I've just been waiting for an excuse like this – and I don't have to play nice now, do I.

I screw my results up in a ball and throw them on the floor as I make my way towards the bogs, rolling my sleeves up ready for a scrap. Another teacher, Mr Thomas, shouts 'Oi you're not allowed in there!' but I barge past him without any trouble.

Mr Mitchell's pissing and must hear me come in but before he can turn all the way round I slam my fist into the back of his head, sending his skull crashing into the wall in front of him, and as his body slumps I'm able to force his face down into the urinal, his own piss, and there's a crunching sound then shouting and someone has hold of me pulling my arms back from behind but I manage to stamp hard on Mr Mitchell's back before being pulled away from the crumpled heap on the floor, and as I'm pinned down by Mr Thomas and another man – I can't see 'cause I'm face down on the floor now – all I can think of is Roger.

Hayley

Just 'cause I wouldn't have sex with him, Mr Mitchell gave me a D.

I can't believe it. I only got four Cs. I look again at my results, trying to count five. No, just four Cs.

I don't know what to do. I'm so angry and feel like I'm going to cry, but everyone's standing round and I can see

170

Jenny Catlow and that lot, and I don't want them to see I'm upset, then Charlie arrives and I can't bear to look at him.

I go to the loo and cry my eyes out, so I don't make a scene, but I end up screaming my head off and slamming my hands against the cubicle and tearing sheets of loo roll off the wall and just proper losing the plot, y'know, then I have a bit of a moment where I stop crying and everything goes quiet, until I hear a girl's voice saying 'Are you OK in there?' and I say back 'Yeah fine!' and she doesn't ask owt again.

When I finally leave I see Mr Mitchell walking towards the staff room. I don't even think about it. I just barge right in after him. Lucky for me, he's the only one in the room.

'Hi Hayley,' he says, a smug look on his face. 'Everything OK?'

'Bastard!' I scream at him, and he gets up and grabs me by my arms, pulling me into him.

I'm suffocating and try to fight back, but he just pulls me closer and I start crying my eyes out on him, then I break free but he yanks me back by my shirt, ripping it.

'I'll tell,' I say, holding my torn shirt. 'You watch.'

'Don't be stupid, Hayley,' he says, grabbing hold of me again before I can get away. 'You ended it. And anyway, look what happened to Sally when she got too big for her boots. She wasn't *ready* either. Well, not with me.' He laughs. 'Now look at her . . . ' I leap forward and take a swing for him, catching him right in the gob, then I burst into tears again but he just laughs.

I storm out, looking a right mess I bet, and Charlie of all people is standing outside. We make eye contact and I try to force a smile, but I lose it again and end up pushing past him.

Then I hear Mr Mitchell come out, and see him walking towards the loos. Charlie stands there for a sec before following Mr Mitchell, then Mr Thomas shouts something but he just ignores him. I run towards them but start to feel silly as the door closes, and there's shouting but I can't really hear what's happening, then Jenny Catlow appears so I slip away.

I just want to disappear, and I'm almost at the doors when I see a piece of paper on the floor. I pick it up to put it in the bin, before realising it's someone's results.

I don't know why but I walk outside, away from Jenny Catlow and everyone, and across the grass to the blossom trees outside the canteen, where all the Sixth Formers sit at dinner. There's nobody there now, though – just me.

I'm still crying and it's raining now. I open the bit of paper and blobs of tears and rain start to blur the typed words. Then I see it's Charlie's results, and I can't believe my eyes.

I stop crying, and start to smile.

CHAPTER TWENTY-FOUR

Russell

I didn't do too badly, after all that. I got what I needed to stay on in Sixth Form anyway, which is OK I suppose. I also got what I needed to go to that college in Leeds. I really don't see how I'll end up going there, unless Mum wins the lottery, but it's still good to know that I got what I wanted, in a way.

I *am* going to a party with Charlie, though. He texted me earlier and asked if I wanted to come, straight after I'd got my results. I don't feel like celebrating staying at that school, I look a mess and my ribs still hurt, but I couldn't really say no could I.

The party's at a girl called Leonie's house. Leonie's one of the popular girls in Year Ten and a really good singer. She even went up for *The X Factor* last year, when the auditions were in Manchester. She got through but then was kicked off, for lying about her age.

Charlie gave me directions. The house is near Duke Bar, where the riots were. Up from Fads across from Coral, he said.

When I get off the bus I walk across the park because it's quicker than walking around. There's this path that goes under the main road, and on the way down it's lined with these really creepy bushes. I walk past and imagine someone hiding in them, waiting for innocent victims to come along.

I emerge from the underpass unscathed and make my

way along the main road, past Fads. As I round the corner I see these Asian lads sitting in a black BMW X5, music blaring. Coral is across the street and I realise I must be near Leonie's. The lads look at me as I pass the car and I start to worry, but then Charlie steps out of a house behind another Asian. I've seen him before, outside school, and think he's a drug dealer. Well, he's probably a drug dealer with a car like that.

Charlie sees me and I smile, then regret it, feeling stupid.

'Hi,' I say, shifting my feet.

'Alreet Russell,' Charlie says, turning to me. I start to think that I'm interrupting, that maybe I shouldn't have bothered coming. 'Look, can you give us a minute? Go inside, grab a can. I'll see you in there, yeah?'

I don't know anyone so I'm a bit reluctant to go inside on my own, even though Brooker and Digger won't be here.

'Don't worry about owt,' he adds, his voice lower now. He's smiling. 'You'll be reet now.'

Inside there are kids everywhere, but I don't recognise any of them from school. They're all about my age and mostly sitting around drinking. The music is too loud, that mind-numbing happy hardcore stuff with a girl singer.

I wander into the kitchen and help myself to a can of Skol from a bucket of cold water that, presumably, used to be ice. Then I walk into the front room, which is full of people all standing around. They've formed a circle. In the centre, a lad's being felt up by two girls – Leonie, and a really skinny blonde with glasses and tiny eyes called Keyra. They're both stroking their hands on him, down his chest, along his stomach and between his legs, and

174

everyone's laughing and shouting.

'He's hard!' Keyra shouts. 'Unlucky pin dick . . . '

'Fuck off!' he says, storming out of the room.

When I turn to leave, sensing that I could be next, Charlie's standing there, holding two cans.

'You're sorted I see . . . ' he says, nodding in the direction of my can.

'Yeah . . . erm, sorry . . . I thought . . . ' I trail off, realising that I don't really know what to say to a lad like Charlie.

'Party's not much crack is it?' he says, after a moment. 'Most of this lot are from round 'ere, though, so what d'you expect?' He laughs. 'Anyway, you want summat stronger? Come wi' me.'

He leads me upstairs and into a back bedroom. A lad I recognise from school, I think his name's Jags, is having sex with a girl against the wardrobe.

'Jog on you two,' says Charlie, sitting down on the bed. They don't mess around, and are gone seconds later. 'Right, I bet you're brickin' it aren't you? I'm sorry to bring you 'ere. I know you don't normally hang round wi' this lot. And I know you get a hard time at school . . . '

'Don't – '

'No,' he interrupts. 'Let me finish. You get a hard time at school, 'specially wi' likes of Brooker and Digger. They're knobs, so it's par f' course, and you won't need to worry about them no more. Anyway, the other day in the cemetery, I started to think there's summat I can do.' He pauses and takes a mouthful of beer, then looks at me. 'Can I ask you a question?' I nod as he downs the rest. 'What d'you want, more than anything?'

175

There's a pause while I think about the question, even though I know the answer already.

'I want to get out of here.'

'I know the feeling. But it's not as simple as that. Not for me anyway . . . '

'What about the exams? I've heard you've done – '

'That won't get me far. D'you think my dad'll pay for university? What wi'? His fuckin' Giro? That's not gonna happen, and even if it could, I don't even wanna go uni anyway.'

'Why?' I ask, confused.

'I'm not like everyone else.'

I laugh, and there's another pause as I realise he's being serious.

'So . . . why did you ask me to come here today?' I say, after that awkward silence. 'What do you need *me* for? I mean, I'm not hard or anything. I couldn't help you . . . you know, do whatever it is you do . . . '

'I could kiss you right now,' he says, smiling.

'I'm not gay, though,' I say, a bit defensively. But it's true. I wouldn't want him thinking that I was.

'I was only jokin'. It's just the way you said that. I'm not comin' on to you or owt, don't worry.'

I look down at my feet, embarrassed, before sipping my can. I don't know what to say, but Charlie just laughs.

'OK,' I say, feeling myself going red, 'so erm . . . why *did* you ask me to come here then?'

'I wanna be mates,' he says, putting his hand in his back pocket, and taking out a brown envelope. He smiles. 'Is that too much to ask?'

Charlie

I fucked up Mr Mitchell pretty bad, but I doubt he'll press charges. I don't give a shit but, put it this way, I wouldn't want any extra attention if I was him.

I'm at Leonie's, even though most people have left, sitting on a bed in the back bedroom. The house was rammed this afternoon. Everyone was on summat – except Russell, who was only here 'cause of me – and I more than likely got it for them. There was the odd line of coke being done in the bathroom, kids on ket, some on vallies 'cause ten mill's only a quid, and a lot of MDMA.

For what it's worth, I don't think it's right to criticise people just for wanting to escape – 'specially when those doing the criticising don't know what the fuck they're talking about. You can't understand unless you're from round 'ere.

But I've started to realise, I'm not cut out for it. All this stuff on the news, the pigs turning up – I'm not ready, and I don't want to take over.

I told Waj and all, when he came round Leonie's earlier. He's off to Manchester tonight and tried to talk me out of it. He even gave me an envelope full of cash, making out like it was a pay rise, but I told him straight.

'I'm not quitting, Waj,' I said, walking him outside. 'I'm just not ready to take all this on . . . '

'I understand, Charlie,' he said, getting back in the X5. 'Will you do one thing for me, though?' He was wearing sunglasses, but turned to look at me.

'Whatever you want, Waj.'

'Meet me at Genesis tonight, before I leave, and we'll

have a drink together. I don't normally touch the stuff, as you know, but this is an exception.'

He drove off, and I went back inside to find Russell. I'd asked him to come 'cause the lad needs a break. He gets a proper hard time at school but I've had my eye on him for a long time now, even though he didn't know it.

Funny thing is, when Waj gave me that envelope I realised I could do more than just look out for him. I've got it all planned out at home, and the Jaguar bag under my bed's full twice over. That extra cash was just burning a fucking hole in my pocket, and I didn't need it.

'What d'you want?' I asked Russell, when we went upstairs.

'I want to get out of here,' he said.

Then I told him everything. About dropping out of school. About my dad. Even about Waj.

'So erm . . . why *did* you ask me to come here then?' he asked.

And I didn't even think about it. Sometimes you just know when summat's right. He needs to get out of here more than anyone, that's for sure, and a few grand'll help him out.

Like I said, though, that's nowt compared to what I've got at home, and nowt compared to what I've got in store for Mum.

Hayley

I'm sitting in our front room with Dad, who's got off work early so he could be at home for when I got my results. He's holding the slip in his hands and I can tell

178

he's disappointed, but he hasn't said owt. Neither of us has said a word since I handed it to him about half an hour ago.

Finally, he puts the results down on the coffee table, and rubs his eyes. He looks tired. I don't think he's been sleeping.

'They said I might be able to go Sixth Form next term, if I do re-sits,' I say, trying to break the silence. Dad's just staring off into space. He doesn't look at me as I speak.

'Well I suppose y'aven't got a choice 'ave yer?' he says, still not looking at me.

'I could get a job . . . '

'Doin' what.' I'm about to answer but then realise it wasn't a question.

'Well I can't do owt about it now can I?' I say, eventually. I must sound frustrated 'cause he just glares at me.

'No yer right, Hayley,' he says. 'It's all too little too late int it? Yer've 'ad chances yer mum and I would've killed for . . . '

'What's Mum got to do wi' owt?' I say, sighing. 'She's dead, remember?'

There's a pause, as I try not to look at him. He stares at me then, after a bit, looks away.

'Can I ask yer a question?' He's lying back on the settee now, his eyes closed.

'Yeah,' I say, knowing exactly what he's about to say.

'Was it worth it?' He opens his eyes and looks straight at me.

I know the answer, but can't bring myself to say it out loud.

CHAPTER TWENTY-FIVE

Russell

My mum's in bed when I get home, just where I left her, but I'm trying not to think too much about that. I floated all the way back from Leonie's. It's as if I've been re-born.

I walk straight into her room and put my results down on the bed, next to where she's propped up watching telly. On the bedside table there are two half-empty canisters of pills and a small wrap, and all around her on the bed are bundles of tissue paper, some of which look to have blood on them. She ignores me and the paper, so I turn the telly off.

'Russell . . . ' she says, slurring, her voice barely audible. 'Put telly . . . back on . . . will yer . . . '

'Don't you want to know how I did?' I ask, standing in front of the telly so I'm in her line of vision.

She doesn't even have to move her head to look at me, but there's no answer. She just stares at the space behind me, as if I'm not here.

'Mum, I have something to tell you, and you're not going to like it . . . ' I continue, walking over to her and sitting on the bed. 'I've decided to go to Leeds, tonight, for the rest of summer. I want to look at going to that college next term, if it's not too late for me to get in.' I put my hand on hers but she doesn't look at me while I speak. She doesn't even look like she's registering what I'm telling her but, after a moment, she opens her mouth, as if to say something.

'Russell . . . ' she says, a tear running down her cheek

and dripping onto the quilt. 'Put telly . . . back on . . . will yer . . . '

Charlie

As soon as I open the back door I can hear shouting.

I run into the front room but it's coming from upstairs, so I climb them fast as I can and barge into my mum and dad's room. He's pinned Mum down on the bed, his hands round her throat.

'Dad get off her!' I scream, climbing on his back. 'Dad – please!'

He's a strong fucker and just shrugs his shoulders, putting me on my back. I jump up and grab hold of his wrists, trying to pull him away from Mum, then I bite his ear, which does the trick.

'Yer gonna tell me what to do in me own 'ouse lad?' he says, wrapping his hands round my neck. 'Who the fuck d'yer think y'are?'

He stinks of drink. I've never seen him this far gone, his face all red, lips dry and chapped. He looks like he's been out for forty-eight hours, which probably isn't far off.

'*Dad . . . please . . .* ' I gasp, tears filling my eyes now, half through fear and half through sheer fucking effort. '*Dad . . .* ' He drops me and I land in front of Mum's dressing table, almost smacking my head on the drawers.

'Right Mother,' he says, dropping his trousers and climbing back on the bed. 'Where was I . . . '

'Dad!' I jump on his back again, wrapping one arm round his neck and grabbing his hair, but he's such a big bastard I can't move him. 'Dad!'

I tug back as hard as I can and the two of us end up falling off the bed together. I roll over and see he's banged his head, and looks in pain.

'Mum come on . . . ' I whisper, trying not to wake him and looking up at the bed.

She gets up, her clothes torn and hanging from her, and staggers out the room behind me.

'Mum . . . ' I say, when we're in my room. I grab the Jaguar bag. 'Look how much money I've got. This is enough for you . . . for you to get away . . . '

Some blood drips from my nose onto the carpet and she comes over, holding her nightie against it, to stop the bleeding. She's got tears in her eyes.

'I've got a plan and everything. I just need to pack you some stuff . . . ' I trail off, realising she's not listening. 'Mum did you hear what I just said? You can have the lot. We can get you a house, far away from him, then – '

'Charlie,' she interrupts, holding her hand to my mouth. 'I can't leave him.' She's crying, but her voice is calm.

'But Mum,' I say, not believing what I'm hearing. 'You can't stay with him. Look at what he's doing to us – to you!'

She shakes her head, then walks away from me, sitting down on my bed.

'Charlie I can't leave him.' She's shivering and starting to rock a bit, losing it, but then she looks right at me. 'I can't. D'you understand? I can't – I *won't*. Please don't make me, Charlie. Don't make me . . . '

'Shush, Mum,' I say, sitting next to her and putting my arm round her waist, to make her stop. 'Shush . . . '

She looks at me again, tears trickling down her face, and reaches out to squeeze my knee, the way she does, when she can't think of owt to say.

I take her hand in mine, without looking at her, and try not to cry.

Hayley

I'm getting ready to go out tonight. I thought Dad wouldn't let me but he didn't seem too bothered when I told him. He's gone out, too, so it doesn't matter now I suppose.

Gemma phoned and begged me to come out with her, 'cause she's got no one else, obviously. I didn't tell her my results, but she told me how well she did – show off.

So I've decided I'm really going for it tonight. I'm only young once and I'll bounce back. I can try Sixth Form next term and do a few re-sits. I'm going to start looking at other Drama courses next term, too.

I haven't told Dad yet, but I think when he calms down a bit he'll forgive me. I don't want him to be disappointed in me – that's the last thing I wanted – but I know I've got some serious making up to do.

I'm glad I didn't go with Mr Mitchell anyway, despite everything. He's used to getting what he wants no matter what happens to everyone else, but I've waited this long for a reason, and I'm not about to be pressured into losing my virginity for one measly A-star.

I put on some mascara and the last dregs of my Bourjois lip gloss, then take a sip of one of Dad's ciders. 'Because the Night' by Patti Smith comes on. Mum used to listen to this before she went out, and I'd watch her getting dressed and putting her makeup on – thinking she was the most beautiful woman in the world. I start singing along, feeling like smiling for the first time in ages, dancing in front of the mirror and hoping Charlie'll be out later, too.

Take me now baby here as I am,
Pull me close, try and understand.
Desire is hunger is the fire I breathe,
Love is a banquet on which we feed.

He might be just a boy, I think, grabbing my hairbrush. But I can still have a bit of fun, can't I?

Because the night belongs to lovers . . .
Because the night belongs to lust . . .
Because the night belongs to lovers . . .
Because the night belongs to us . . .

CHAPTER TWENTY-SIX

Hayley

I wake up in my room, and everything's quiet. It's like I've slept for days and I'm proper groggy but also a bit, I dunno. I get up, slowly, and go to the loo. It burns when I pee, but my headache's worse – a lot worse.

I can only remember bits of last night, but I do know I couldn't believe it when I saw Charlie. He looked awful, like he'd been in a fight.

He might be scared, I remember thinking when we went to the bar, but maybe we could be friends and, in time, who knows what else. We chatted for a bit, but it was hard to hear him 'cause the music was so loud.

I make my way downstairs, thinking it all got a bit blurry after that. The house feels cold, like someone's died, and I'm still tired and reckon I might just go straight back to bed with a brew.

When I walk into the kitchen I see Dad at the table. He looks up and smiles, but he doesn't look happy. I hope he's not still mad at me about my results, I think, putting the kettle on. Well I hope he's less mad anyway.

'Don't worry about that sweet 'eart,' he says. 'I've got a fresh pot 'ere . . . '

I sit down across from him and he starts possin'.

'How are yer feelin'?' he says, after a bit. He looks like he's been crying, and I start to think he'll never forgive me at this rate.

185

'Erm . . . OK, just a bit tired maybe. What's wrong, Dad? You're not still mad at me are you?' I reach across the table to touch his hand, but he gets up and walks over to the fridge.

'D'yer want milk?'

'Dad the milk's here,' I say, pouring myself a cup and holding the milk up, so he can see it.

He sits back down and doesn't say owt else.

I stir my tea and start to remember a bit more about last night. It's not clear, just flashes, but I know I was talking to Charlie at the bar, then he got dragged away by one of his Paki mates. The older one, I think. I don't know his name. I must've just waited by the VIP, where they were sitting. I know Gemma kept trying to get me back on the dancefloor, but I wanted to be near Charlie.

'What's the matter, Dad?' I say, sipping my tea. My mouth tastes funny, and I think I've cut my lip. I try and look in a spoon, but can't see properly. 'You're not acting yourself . . . '

He looks at me but still doesn't speak.

'Dad will you please tell me what's goin' on?'

'What d'yer remember about last night?' he says, dead serious.

When he asks this there's a flash of me and Charlie, in the VIP bit, and we're both laughing.

'I understand,' he carries on. 'They said it could take a few days, y'know, for it all to come back – '

'Who are *they*?' I interrupt.

'The doctors.' He looks down at his tea and starts stirring in lumps of sugar, even though he's put at least three in already.

'The doctors?' I ask, confused.

He gets up again to put his mug in the sink. 'Yer'd a bit of an . . . *accident* . . . last night . . . ' He trails off, and doesn't look at me.

'What kind of accident? I feel fine – '

'I thought yer'd had too much t' drink,' he interrupts, turning to look at me. 'And I were mad when they told me you just got dumped in A&E by that bloody taxi driver . . . ' He shakes his head. 'I dint know, though . . . '

'A taxi driver? Wait, didn't know what?'

'I got a call saying yer'd needed yer stomach pumped, but only 'cause yer drink'd been spiked. They found summat in yer system, when they did their checks . . . '

'I . . . erm . . . I don't understand . . . ' I say, trying to remember, but I'm only getting bits and pieces and nowt makes sense.

I can see a door at the back of the club, with a bouncer in front of it.

I can see a long corridor that I don't think is in the club, then some stairs, maybe a basement, I'm not sure.

And I can see a light swinging above my head, and it's like I'm lying down, sleeping, but with my eyes open.

'Hayley,' Dad says, snapping me out of it. He's sitting across from me at the table now. 'I need yer t' try and remember what happened last night, who yer were wi' and – '

'I can't, Dad,' I interrupt, starting to panic. 'I'm trying, but I can't remember it all . . . '

Then in a flash I see Charlie's face, and he kisses me – he

definitely kisses me. It's soft, though, gentle. A bit like a dream.

'The police'll 'ave some questions, but I can tell 'em t' wait a few days if that's better.' He reaches out to touch my hand, but I pull it away.

'What d'you mean, *police*? What have they got to do with it? I didn't do owt wrong . . . '

'Hayley, please – '

'I only had a few drinks, *God!*' I stand up and start to walk out the kitchen.

'Hayley come back . . . '

'I'm tired, Dad, I just need – '

'Hayley I'm sorry!' he screams, before I get to the door.

I stop, then turn round. He puts his head in his hands, staring down at the table, and starts to cry.

'I'm so sorry sweet 'eart. I'm so, so sorry . . . '

Charlie

Who am I? I'm a lover not a fighter. A techno fiend.

Where am I? I'm in Genesis, making my way down to the dancefloor.

> *Love is . . .*
> *Love is . . .*
> *Love is . . .*

The baseline of the music hits as I push my way through the crowd.

> *Love is . . . gone, gone, gone . . .*

Then the beat kicks in as I cross the floor and someone touches my cheek and I'm sweating but not cold, my eyes filled with tears.

Waj hasn't turned up yet so I get a drink, and end up bumping into Hayley at the bar. Just my luck. I smile and nod as she goes on, thinking she probably knows I pasted Mr Mitchell – and I know about them. She offers to buy me a drink but I shake my head, then I see Waj. He spots us and comes over, introducing himself to Hayley, before telling me to follow.

We go in the VIP, cut off from everyone else, and he signals for some girl to bring us a bottle of summat. I can see Hayley hovering in the background, but ignore her.

'When you off to Manchester?' I say, struggling to speak over the music.

'Sorry?' he says, not looking at me.

'I said, when you leavin'?'

The waitress comes and starts pouring us both a drink. All the time she's pouring, Waj is staring at me. I try to keep eye contact, but there's summat about him that's fucking freaking me out. He's got that menace in his eye, like the time with the junky, in that pub.

'Have a drink,' he says, handing me a glass.

'I don't fancy it – '

'Cheers!' he says, shoving the drink into my chest and spilling some on my shirt. He clinks his glass against mine, then downs it.

Some underage girls come over and sit either side of him. I take that as my cue.

'Alreet Waj,' I say, already starting to stand. 'Suppose I'll be off then. See you tomorrow? I'll come down Power – '

'Sit the fuck down,' he says, not looking at me.

I just stand there, not sure what to do.

'Didn't you hear me?' he says, now looking straight at me. The girls don't seem to notice, just staring gormlessly round the club. 'I said, sit the – '

'Fuck you.'

I don't even think about it and walk straight out the VIP, barging into a clean shirt trying to get behind the rope. Hayley's still standing there and all, but I just blank her.

There's no way I'm putting up with that shit. I'm fucking furious and want to punch something, or someone, but at the same time I don't feel like I've got owt left. I get outside and walk down the street, stopping in front of the taxi rank and looking in my pockets for a cigarette. I'm sober and everything feels different, strange, 'specially at this time of night.

Then I feel a hand on my shoulder. I turn round, and see it's Waj.

'I'm sorry about that, Charlie,' he says, my best mate all of a sudden. 'Are you OK?'

'What's your problem? I told you I'm not quittin', Waj. I'm just not ready for it . . . '

'It doesn't work like that, Charlie,' he says, shaking his head. 'Do you think you can pick and choose, dip in and out, now that you're involved? I don't think so.'

'But earlier, when I said I didn't wanna take it on – '

'I've thought about it,' he interrupts, helping himself to the fag in my hand, 'and, ready or not, I want to make something clear.' He lights it then exhales to his right. 'I need you to take over. You're too precious to me, and I can't let you go . . . '

'I said I'm not quittin', Waj. I don't understand – '

'Well understand this,' he says, blowing smoke in my face, 'you're a tough lad, Charlie, but I'm in charge – so don't fuck with me.' He grabs me by the shirt and shoves me, hard, against the wall of the club.

'Waj, stop . . . ' I say, trying to shrug him off. He's fucking strong, though, and just holds me there. 'Get the fuck off!' I shout, managing to push past, but before I can get anywhere he spins me round and shoves me back against the wall, pinning me there.

'I expected you to behave like this,' he says, his voice low. 'And I knew you wouldn't take it well . . . '

'What the fuck are you doin', Waj?' I say, struggling to breathe let alone break free.

'I always knew that you were loyal, Charlie.' He shoves me back against the wall so my head smacks the concrete, and I take a swing for him but he dodges and lamps me, square in the nose, knocking me down. 'Your problem is you think too much,' he says, picking me up and leading me away from the taxi rank.

He drags me by my collar down an alley, and throws me into some bins. I scramble to my feet, and see his X5.

'You need to know your place – and understand what happens when I don't get what I want. You remember Asif?'

I look at Waj, tears streaming down my face now, as he opens the boot and motions for me to come over.

'I own you, Charlie,' he says, smiling as I look inside the open sports bag. It's a face I recognise, with shaved eyebrows.

And no body.

'Don't worry, Charlie,' he says, slamming it shut. His voice is completely different now – calm. He puts his arm back round me and grips the back of my neck. 'I'm not going to hurt you. Just remember one thing, OK?'

I look at him, even though I can barely stand I'm so scared, and nod.

'I don't do second chances.'

He leads me back into the club, across the dancefloor to the VIP. I see Hayley still hovering, and Waj opens the rope for her. Then we all sit back down, like outside never happened.

I'm in a daze but Waj is just like his old self, surrounded by girls, drinks flowing. I don't know what else to do but drink, and it's not long before I start to feel pissed – letting the whole thing wash over me, like it had to be this way all along.

Hayley's on at me in my ear, even more of a lightweight than me. I don't resist her, even when she starts putting her hands on my leg. I'm that far gone now, I don't give a shit. She laughs at everything I say, everything Waj says and all, and pretty soon I feel a menace – back to *my* old self.

Waj treats me like normal, after a bit, and gets matier with every drink. He knows, like I do, I'm going nowhere.

'Here you go,' he says, bringing us the biggest fucking cocktail I've ever seen. 'For the two lovers.'

'Thanks Waj, you shouldn't of,' she says, drunk. I laugh – at her, not with her – but she thinks I'm being friendly so just smiles.

A bit of that and she's falling all over me, starting to lose it. I don't want any 'cause it looks rank, and I'm starting to think about getting rid of her by now – I've had enough – so I stand up and lead her out the VIP. The dancefloor's rammed, though, and I can't see an exit.

I put my arm round her before she passes out completely and take her to the back of the club, where Kaz the Albanian bouncer shows us out – and to the back door.

On the way she stumbles, giggles, and when I pick her up she kisses me. It's more of a slobber than a kiss but we look at each other, then she starts to drift, muttering summat about being drunk.

'No shit, Sherlock . . . '

Kaz, who's massive and covered in tattoos – even some on his head, which is shaved down to the bone – keeps us moving as we walk through a door and a long corridor, then down some stairs. I can't see any back door, just a light swinging above us, and it takes a bit for my eyes to adjust.

Next minute, I see Kaz standing at the top of the stairs again, and he just grins, closing the door and standing in front of it – so nobody can get through.

The light above my head's making me have to squint, and I look back at Hayley, on the bottom step, and see she's got no knickers on – her skirt round her waist. I've no fucking idea where we are, and try and pick her up again. Then she kisses me – she definitely kisses me – but this time it's soft, gentle, my hands on her bare legs.

'What d'you want?' I say, kissing her neck without thinking. I can't help myself, falling down and pushing myself into her.

She moans, then mutters summat again – I think, 'I love you.'

It happens fast. I kiss her hard on the mouth, biting her lip, unzipping and trying to get her wet – but she's too out of it for that. I don't stop, though, and slide a finger inside. She feels too tight, but then I lift up her legs and push against her. When I pull out, I see there's blood.

She'd probably reckon I was doing her a favour, I'm thinking, going all the way back in, my head buzzing. Better me than some other lad. Or that cunt, Mr Mitchell.

She slumps on the floor when I'm finished, her eyes closed, but I'm sobering up and spinning out. I start to think I should sort her out, so pull her skirt up then tidy her hair, to make it look like she's not just been fucked on some stairs. Then I take her out the back and put her in a taxi.

I walk across town on autopilot, needing to clear my head, but I can barely take owt in. I pass Planet Pizza, which is filling up, then the bandstand and McDonald's, and towards the multi-storey.

It's raining, but I'm soon inside the car park and making my way up to the top level. There's this homeless man sleeping by the steps on level three and I think of that night in Manchester, and how no matter what they do to dress it up round 'ere will always be the same. I take out what cash I have, £100, and slip it under his sleeping bag.

When I get to the top I look out across town, the climax of another night. I can see Hollywood Park, just a big red stripe, the Turf, the floodlights still on from tonight's match, and fucking useless chimneys everywhere you look.

194

I can cope with me, I think to myself as I look down. It's everyone else I want to escape from.

Russell

I've just told Jason that I'm on my way, and even though it's a bit last minute and getting late he seemed really happy. I'm on the train now, waiting to set off while listening to another song by that band he told me about. It's called 'Let's Start'.

There was over five grand in the envelope that Charlie gave to me earlier. I put half in a shoe box and left it for Mum on top of the toilet seat, so even she couldn't miss it. I can use what's left to get myself started, then get a job. That's the plan anyway, but I suppose I'll just have to wait and see.

Looking out of the window as the sun goes down and another night begins, I can see the whole town bathed in a sanguine light. I can see the cinema and the bright red beam that cuts across its façade, and the football stadium that's lit up for tonight's match. I can see the town hall too, and the tall chimneys that have framed this place for decades.

> *We should start,*
> *Fallin' apart.*
> *We're fallin' apart,*
> *And heaven knows, we're better off alone . . .*

There's a kind of radiance about the town in an evening, which I've never noticed until now. It's almost as if the town is vibrating, buzzing with oranges, reds, yellows and whites.

And after all the injury,
Nothin' means that much to me.
Let's start, fallin' apart,
You'll be fallin' with me.

As the train pulls away from the platform I press my hand, then face, against the cold glass of the window.

I've spent most of my life wanting to escape, just waiting for this day.

Now I'm finally doing it, and I didn't expect to feel this way.

Acknowledgements

I'd like to thank Quartet Books, especially Naim Attallah and David Elliott.

Mum and Dad – for continuing to back me and this, my dreadful mistake.

Andrew Bower, Philip Hatfield, Nikesh Shukla – and everyone with something to say about *Made in Britain*, good or bad.

Carl Davis – for nailing the jacket (again).

And Sophie – for the fire, and for being my best friend. Always.

Acknowledgements